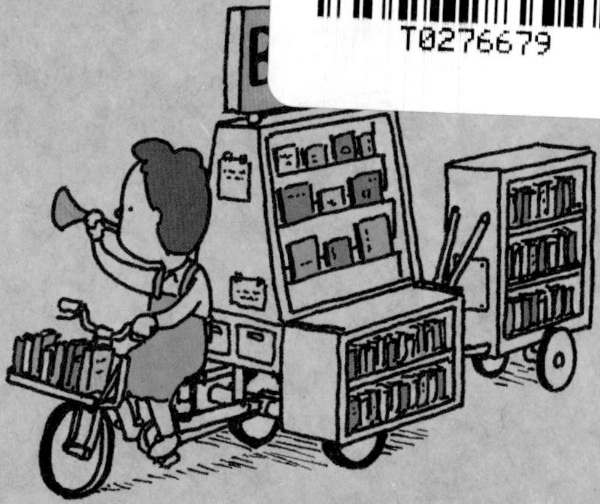

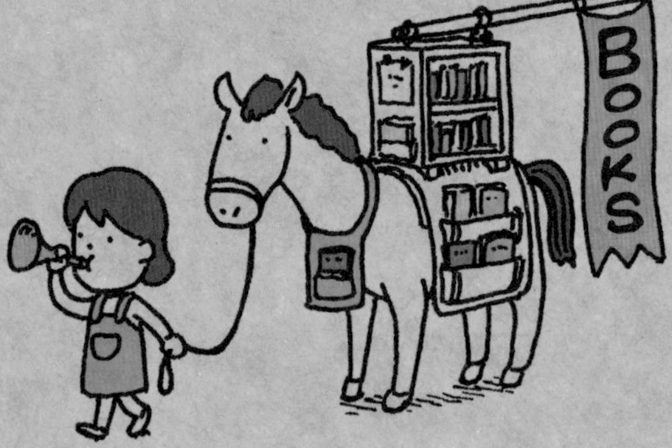
BOOKS

THE
I WONDER
BOOKSTORE

Shinsuke Yoshitake

CHRONICLE BOOKS
SAN FRANCISCO

The I Wonder Bookstore is located in the far corner of town.

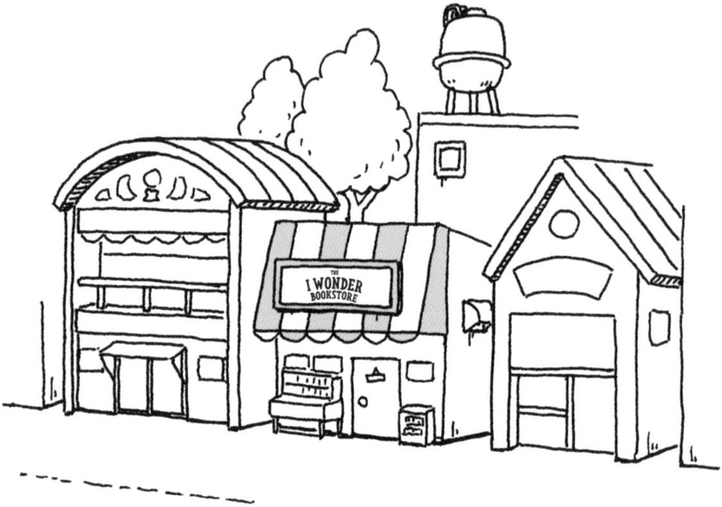
THE
I WONDER
BOOKSTORE

This bookstore only sells books about books.

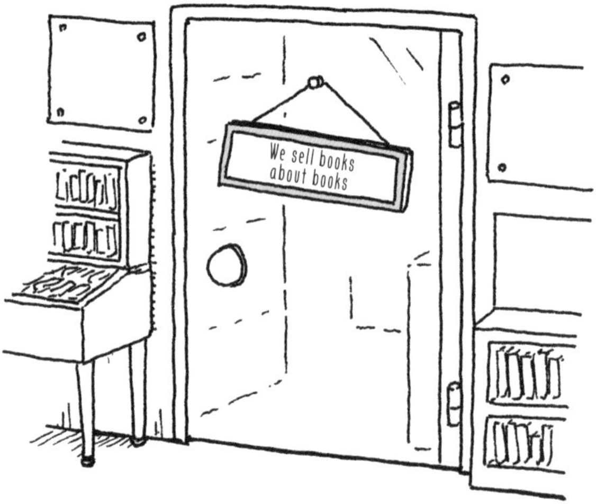
We sell books
about books

If you ask the man in the store,
"I wonder if you have any books about...?"

He usually says, "Uh-huh! Yes we do!" and retrieves
some books from the back of the store.

Today, like any other day, customers will come
to the I Wonder Bookstore looking for special
books of all kinds.

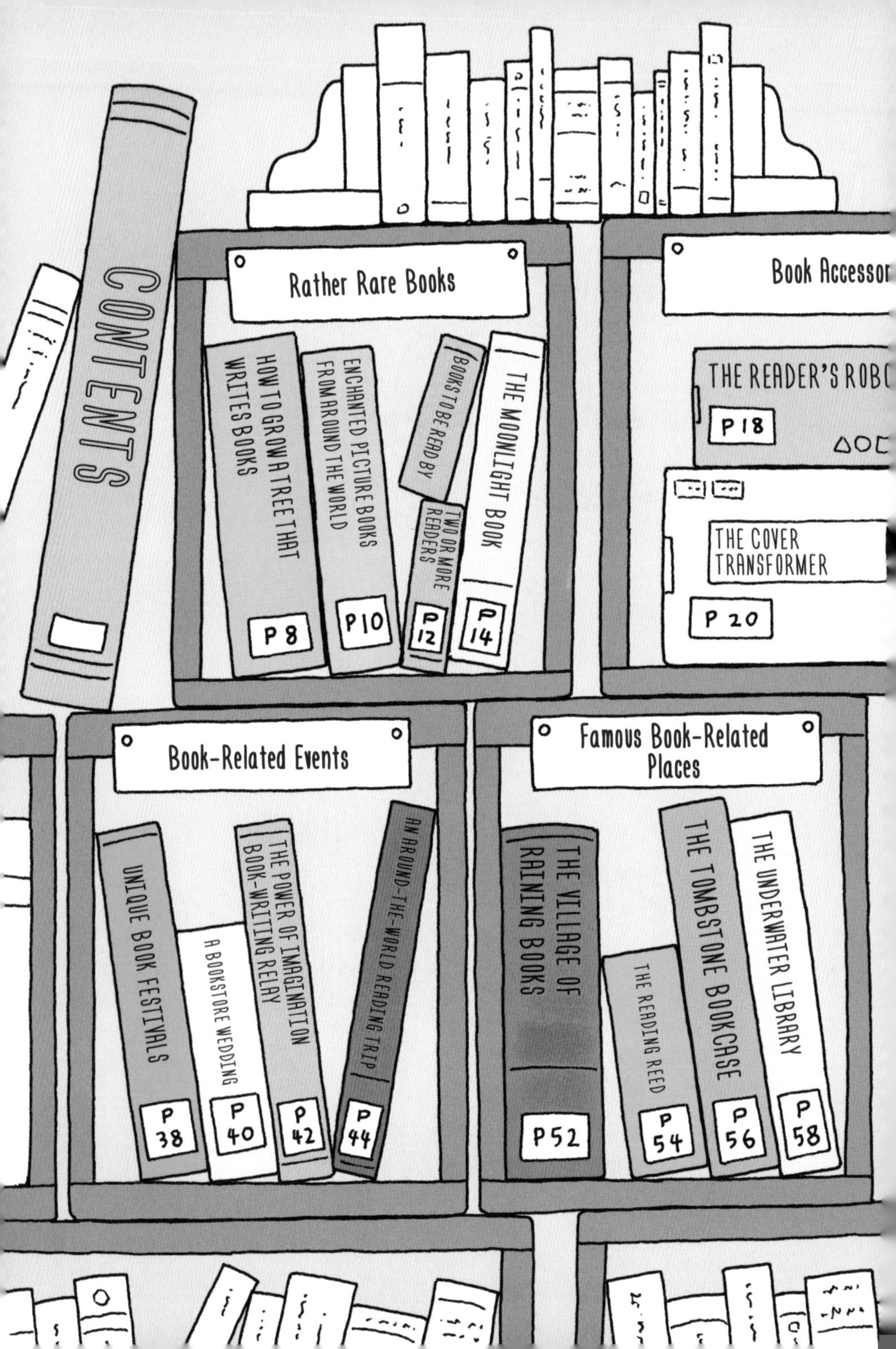
CONTENTS
Rather Rare Books
HOW TO GROW A TREE THAT WRITES BOOKS
P 8
ENCHANTED PICTURE BOOKS FROM AROUND THE WORLD
P10
BOOKS TO BE READ BY
TWO OR MORE READERS
P 12
THE MOONLIGHT BOOK
P 14
Book Accessor
THE READER'S ROBO
P 18
THE COVER TRANSFORMER
P 20
Book-Related Events
UNIQUE BOOK FESTIVALS
P 38
A BOOKSTORE WEDDING
P 40
THE POWER OF IMAGINATION BOOK-WRITING RELAY
P 42
AN AROUND-THE-WORLD READING TRIP
P 44
Famous Book-Related Places
THE VILLAGE OF RAINING BOOKS
P52
THE READING REED
P 54
THE TOMBSTONE BOOKCASE
P 56
THE UNDERWATER LIBRARY
P 58

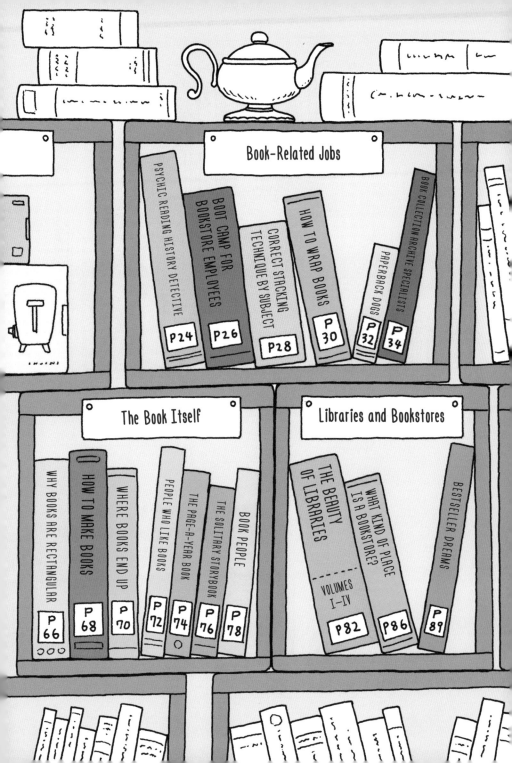

Book-Related Jobs

PSYCHIC READING HISTORY DETECTIVE — P24

BOOT CAMP FOR BOOKSTORE EMPLOYEES — P26

CORRECT STACKING TECHNIQUE BY SUBJECT — P28

HOW TO WRAP BOOKS — P30

PAPERBACK DOGS — P32

BOOK COLLECTION ARCHIVE SPECIALISTS — P34

The Book Itself

WHY BOOKS ARE RECTANGULAR — P66

HOW TO MAKE BOOKS — P68

WHERE BOOKS END UP — P70

PEOPLE WHO LIKE BOOKS — P72

THE PAGE-A-YEAR BOOK — P74

THE SOLITARY STORYBOOK — P76

BOOK PEOPLE — P78

Libraries and Bookstores

THE BEAUTY OF LIBRARIES — VOLUMES I–IV — P82

WHAT KIND OF PLACE IS A BOOKSTORE? — P86

BESTSELLER DREAMS — P89

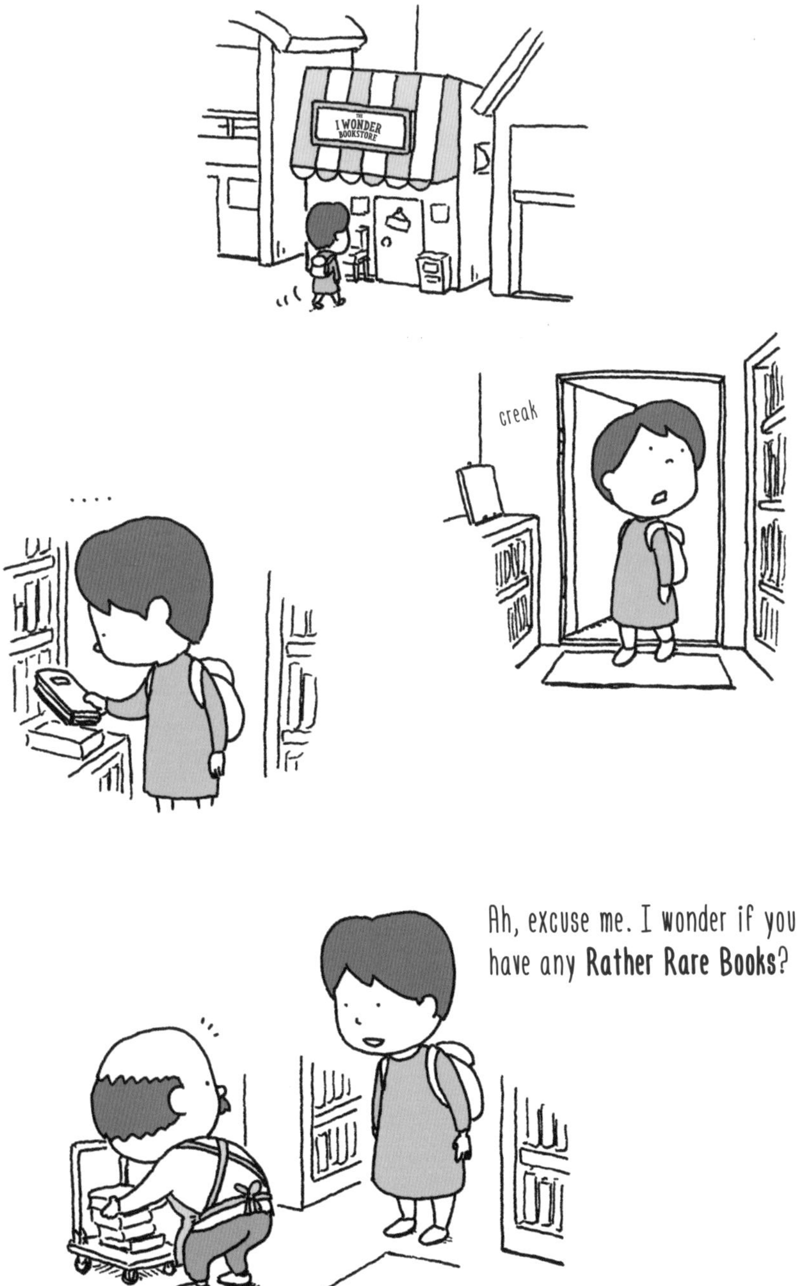
THE I WONDER BOOKSTORE
creak
....
Ah, excuse me. I wonder if you have any **Rather Rare Books**?

Uh-huh!
Yes we do!

Now let me see . . .

How about these?

Please let me
tell you
about them . . .

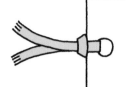

"HOW TO GROW A TREE THAT WRITES BOOKS"

1. Place a seed in between the pages of your favorite book and bury it in the ground.

2. Every day, nurture it with care by reading it many different books.

3. Each year, when it is "book fall" season, the books ripen.
   Some trees take several years before bearing fruit.

4. If you nurture the tree with great care,
   then it will produce good books.

Oh boy, this mystery is a
once-in-ten-years masterpiece!

5. However, if you carelessly praise
   another tree, yours will
   sulk and stop bearing fruit.

Oh no!

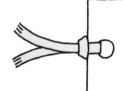

"ENCHANTED PICTURE BOOKS FROM AROUND THE WORLD"

the pop-up book

the melt-down book

the run-away book

the chow-down book

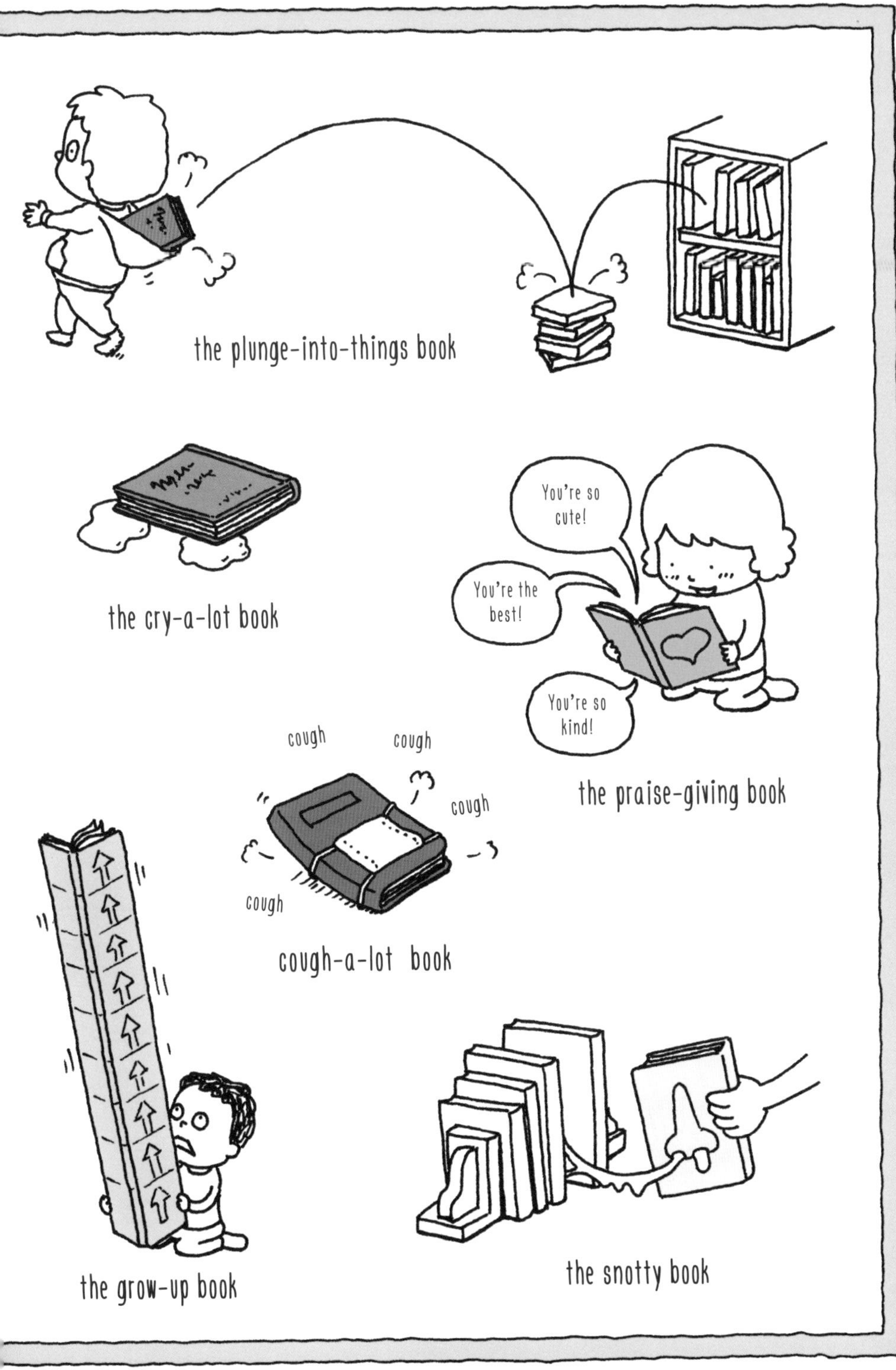

the plunge-into-things book
the cry-a-lot book
You're so cute!
You're the best!
You're so kind!
the praise-giving book
cough
cough
cough
cough
cough-a-lot book
the grow-up book
the snotty book

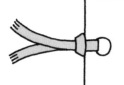

"BOOKS TO BE READ BY TWO OR MORE READERS"

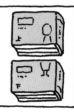

1. This book is divided into a top volume and bottom volume.

2. Each only contains half the story, so you have to turn the pages together to read the full story.

One fine day she thought she might take her dog Lucky

Top volume

to the park for a walk. When they got there,

Bottom volume

3. The book is designed to be read like this, by two people together.

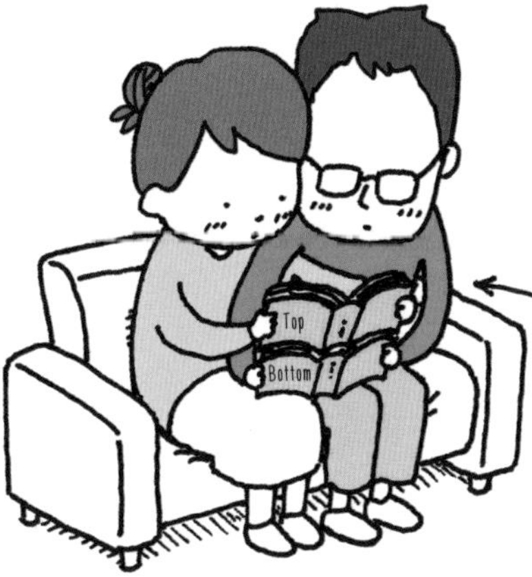
Top
Bottom

"Lovers" two-volume set

4. The concept is also popular in office settings.

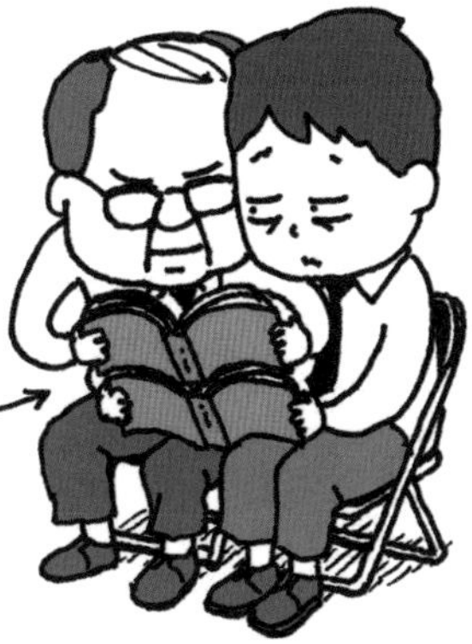

"Ideal Relations between Managers and Junior Employees" two-volume set

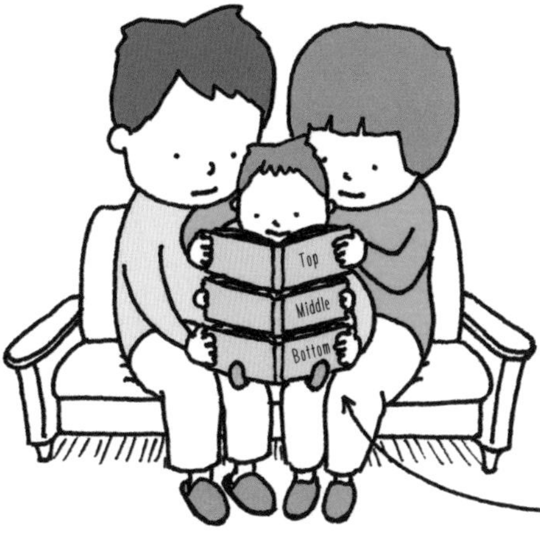
Top
Middle
Bottom

5. A "Special Family Edition" (with top, middle, and bottom volumes) is also available.

"Three on a Journey" three-volume set

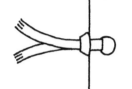

"THE MOONLIGHT BOOK"

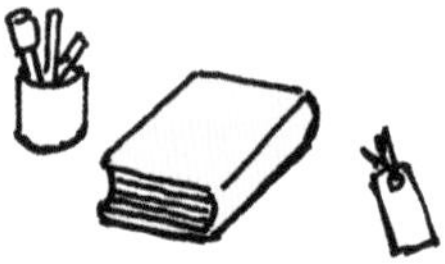

1. This book is printed in a special luminous ink only visible under moonlight, developed by accident about 70 years ago.

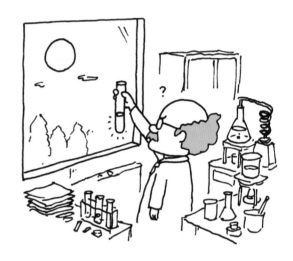

2. This means that the pages all seem white and blank in daylight or under electric lights.

Yep, can't see a thing!

Oh!
Hmm, the sky m
be clear tonight

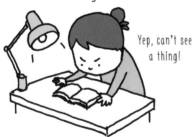

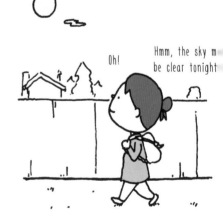

3. You can only read the book on a clear night under a full moon.

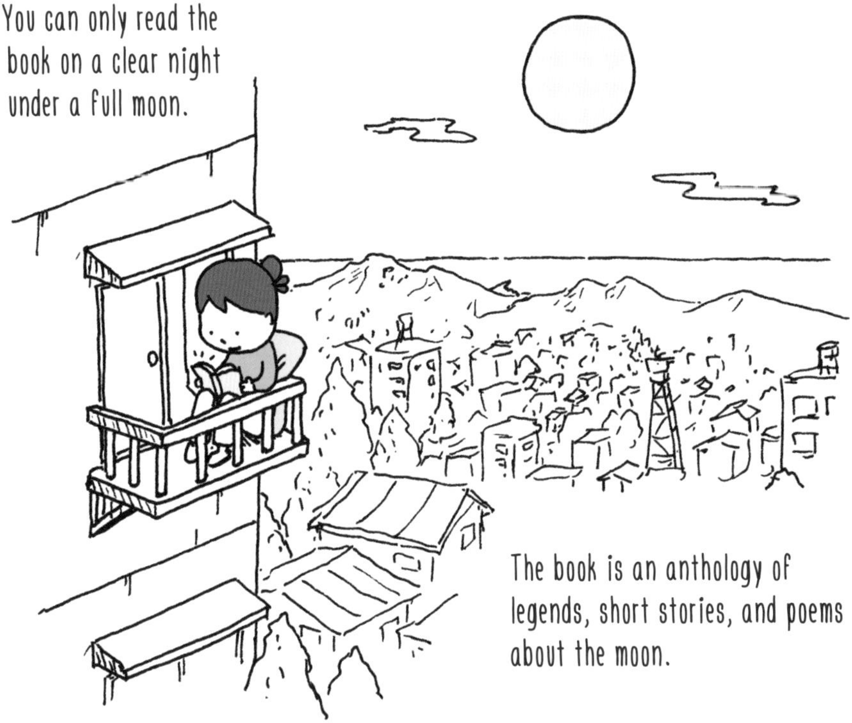

The book is an anthology of legends, short stories, and poems about the moon.

4. You can also use a pen filled with the same special ink (sold separately) to write down things to be read only by moonlight.

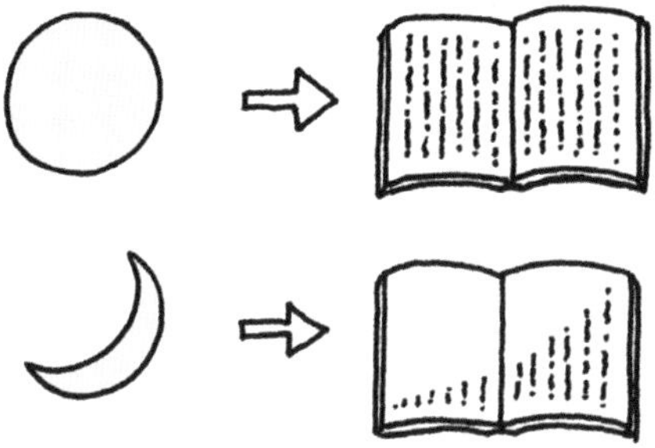

5. Some of the text can be read under a crescent moon, but not as much.

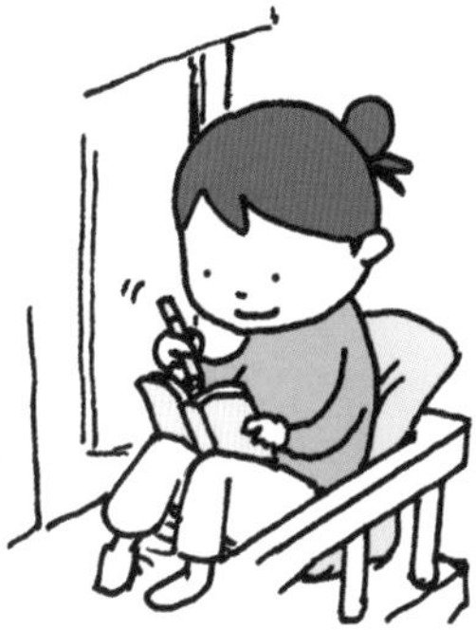

Hmm.

Okay, I'll take this book, please.

Thank you!

Right, now where was I ...

Um. Hello.
Could you help me?

Oh. Yes, of course. How can I help?

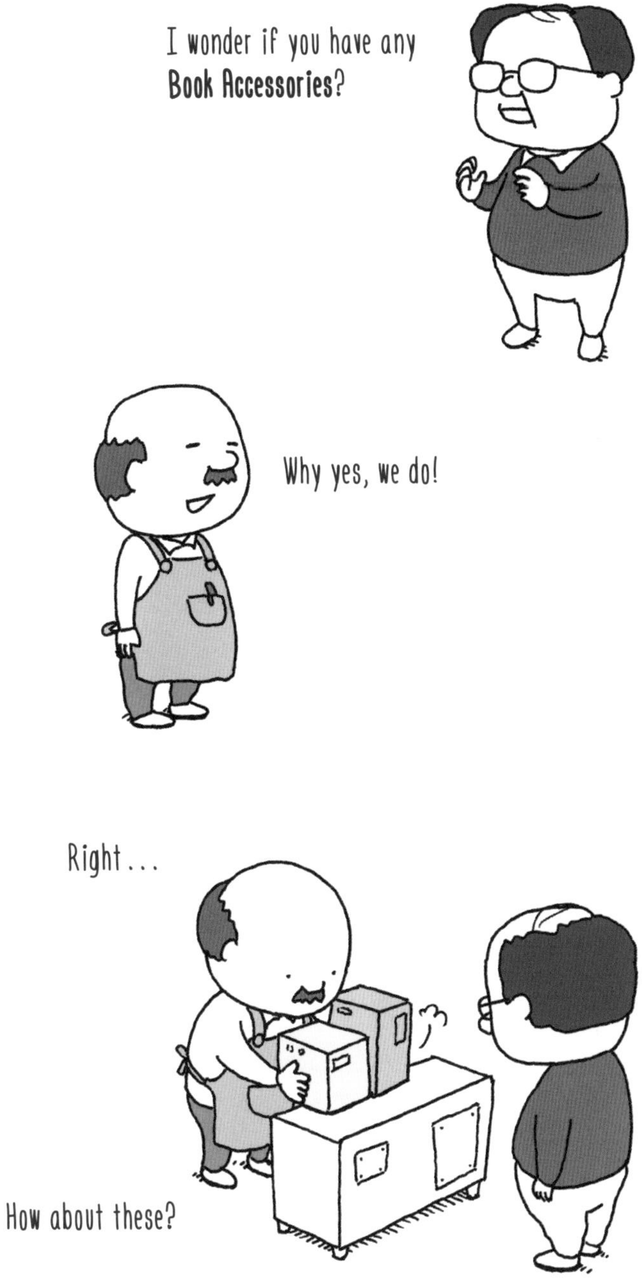
I wonder if you have any
Book Accessories?
Why yes, we do!
Right . . .
How about these?

"THE READER'S ROBOT"

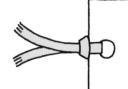

To enhance your reading experience!

The brand-new Reader's Robot

It has lots of useful features!

⭐ It plugs your ears in a noisy room.

⭐ It encourages you.

You've read so far already!

You're almost at the end!

It warns you not to read in a room that is too dark.

 It wakes you if you nod off.

You'll ruin your eyes!!

Hey!

You'll damage the book!

It asks what you think about your book.

It serves as your bookmark.

I see . . .

Well maybe you'll find it interesting in ten years' time?

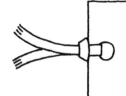

"THE COVER TRANSFORMER"

1. When a friend is coming over on short notice, and you are embarrassed by all the low-brow books in your house...

...just insert those books in this machine...

Get Rich Quick

Ka-ching!

Efficient Wealth Generation

Whirrr . . .
Buzz Buzz Buzz Buzz

...and it will change your book's title and cover to make you seem more intelligent.

2. You can choose the style and subject for your new cover design.

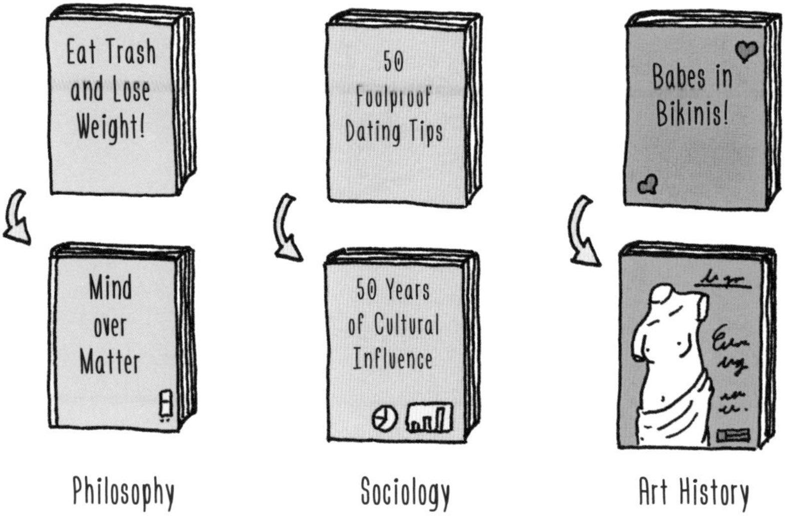
Eat Trash and Lose Weight!
Mind over Matter
Philosophy
50 Foolproof Dating Tips
50 Years of Cultural Influence
Sociology
Babes in Bikinis!
Art History

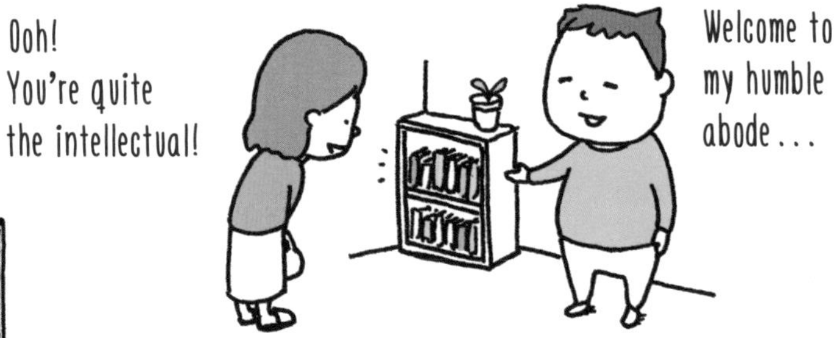
Ooh! You're quite the intellectual!
Welcome to my humble abode . . .

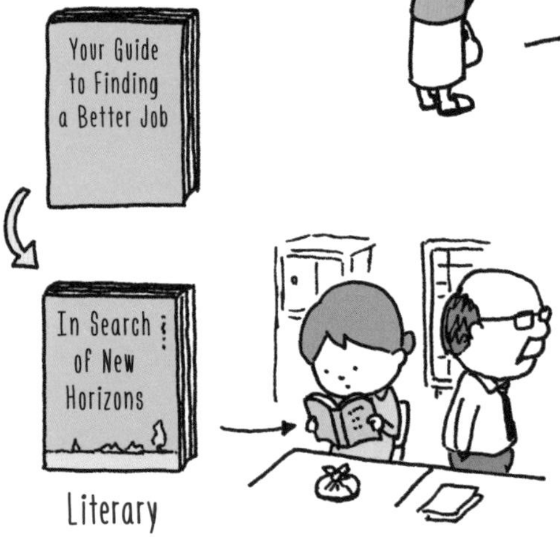
Your Guide to Finding a Better Job
In Search of New Horizons
Literary

3. It is also effective for books that are too embarrassing to read in public.

Please come again!

Right then...
where was I?

Oh . . . yes?

Ahem . . .

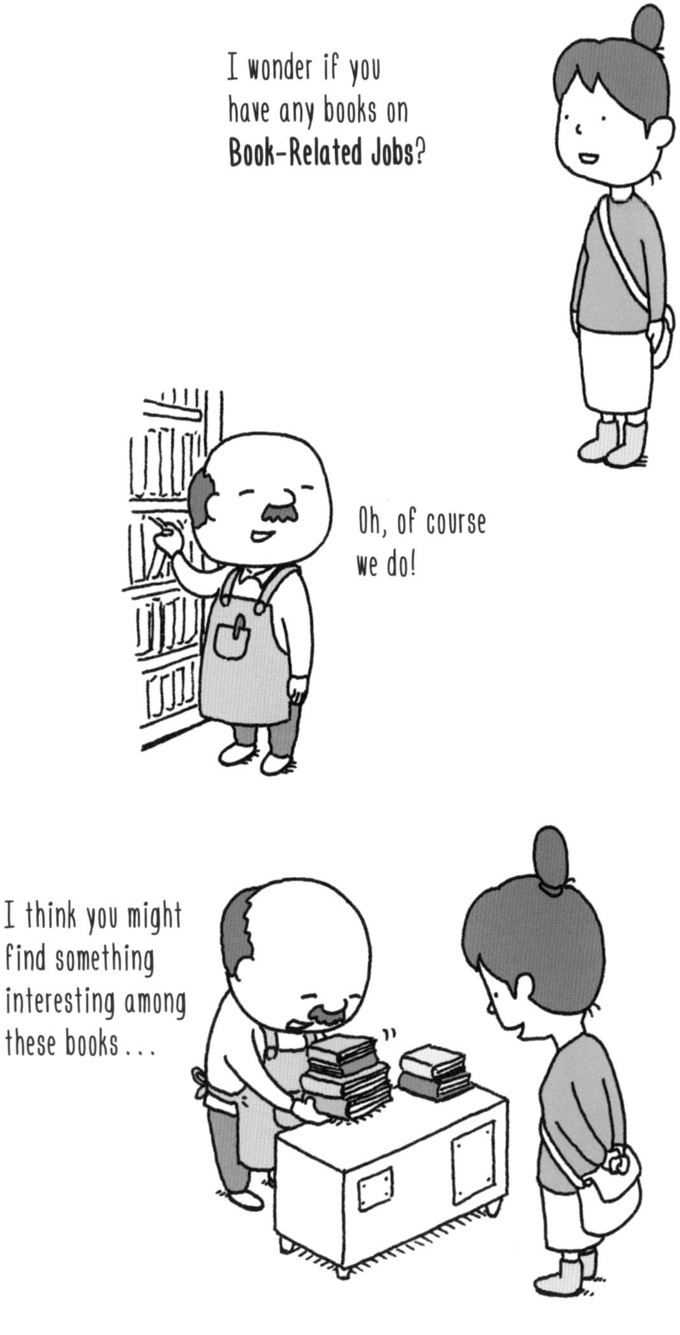
I wonder if you have any books on **Book-Related Jobs**?
Oh, of course we do!
I think you might find something interesting among these books . . .

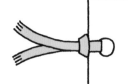

"PSYCHIC READING HISTORY DETECTIVE"

He solves cases through the psychic ability of knowing what books the suspect has read up until now.

I can see his bookcase...

How did you know I would be here?

Last month you read *100 Beautiful Coastal Views.*

Drat...!

I have the power to see all the books you have read.

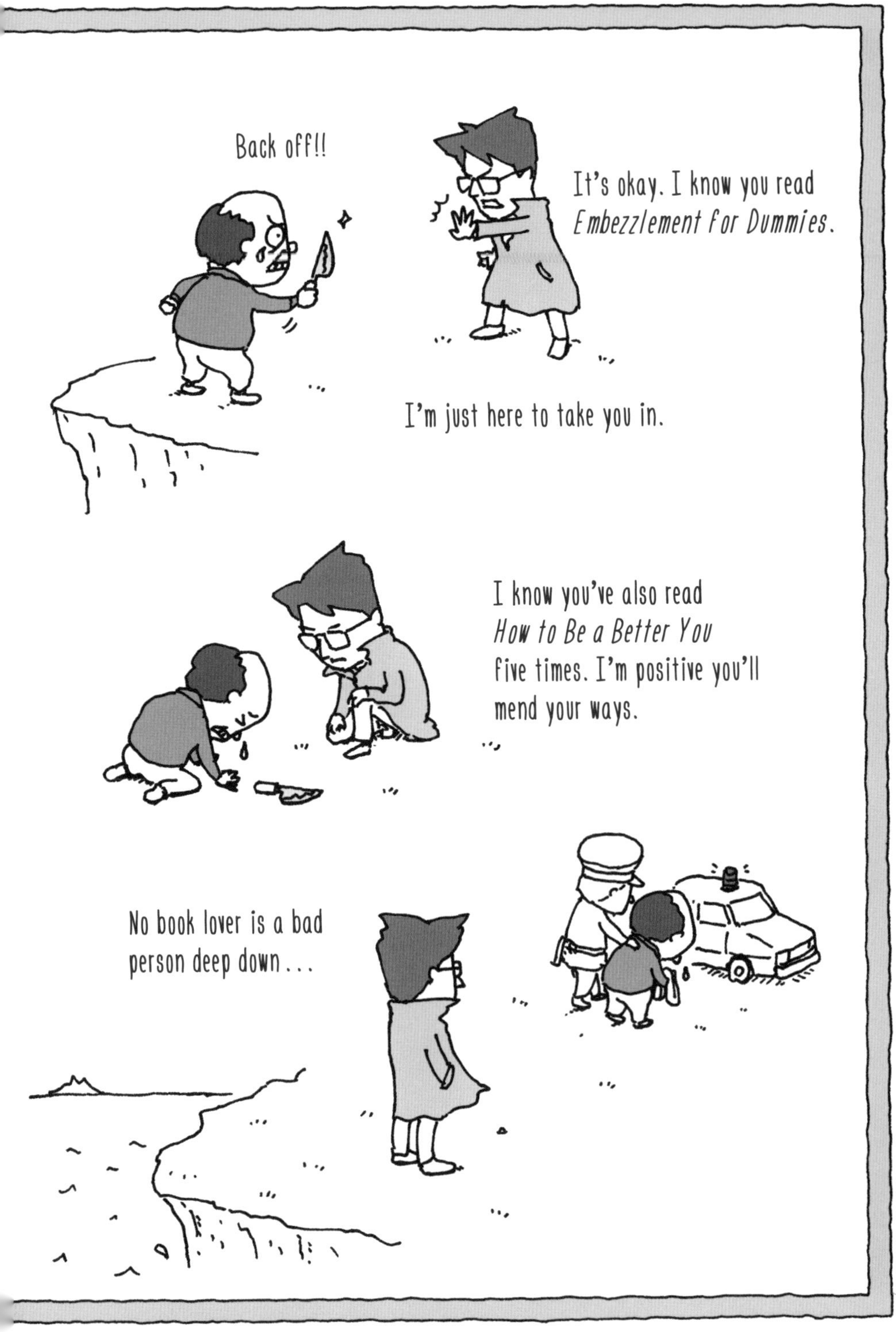

Back off!!
It's okay. I know you read *Embezzlement for Dummies*.
I'm just here to take you in.
I know you've also read *How to Be a Better You* five times. I'm positive you'll mend your ways.
No book lover is a bad person deep down...

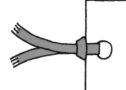

"BOOT CAMP FOR BOOKSTORE EMPLOYEES"

5:30 a.m. Rise and shine

6:30 a.m. Aerobics

7:00 a.m. Breakfast / Cart marathon

9:00 a.m. Blindfolded archival jacket wrapping

1:00 p.m. Lunch/Book balancing while reviewing purchase orders

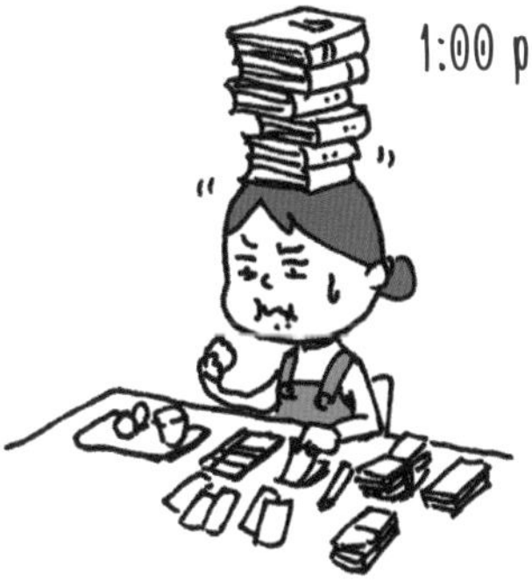

4:00 p.m. Book-sorting drills: by release date, by alphabetical order, and by popularity

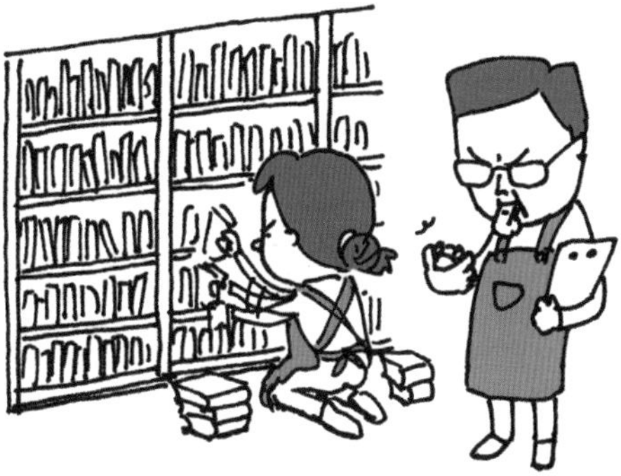

7:00 p.m. Dinner/Shelf-talker writing (using a weighted pen)

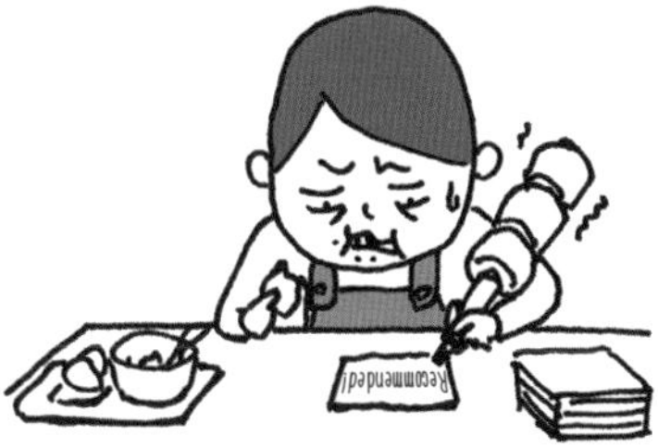
Recommended!

9:00 p.m. Free time

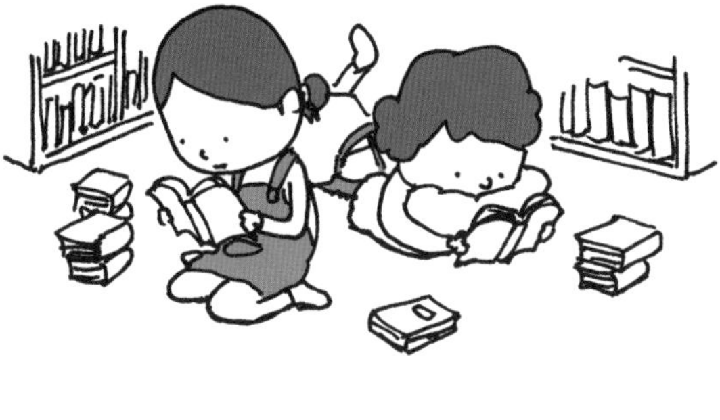

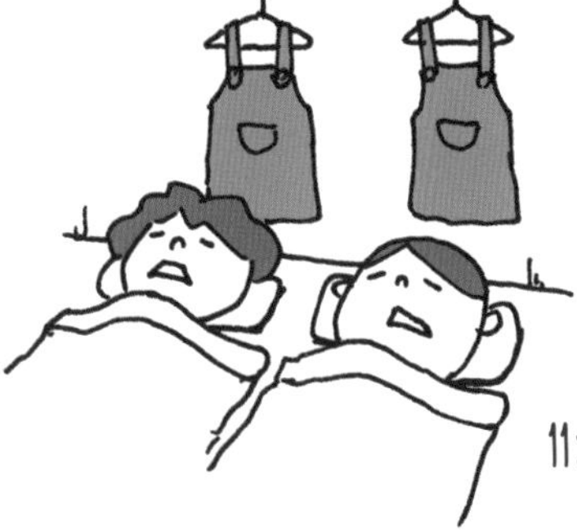

11:00 p.m. Sleep

Bookstore Employee Skill-Builder Series

"CORRECT STACKING TECHNIQUE BY SUBJECT"

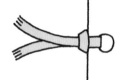

Political Instability Now
six-volume set

Practical Application of Structural Engineering
nine-volume set

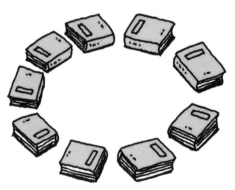

The Social Benefit of Recycling
nine-volume set

Easy Outdoor Living
five-volume set

Yoga for Families
parent and child edition

*The Domino Effect in
Modern History*
28-volume set

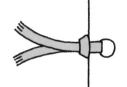

Bookstore Employee Skill-Builder Series
"HOW TO WRAP BOOKS"
I'll take this one, please.
Thank you kindly!
Do you need a bag, or shall I wrap it specially for you?...
Gift wrapped
Plain paper bag
Time capsule
Twine (for after you've "tied one on")

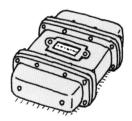

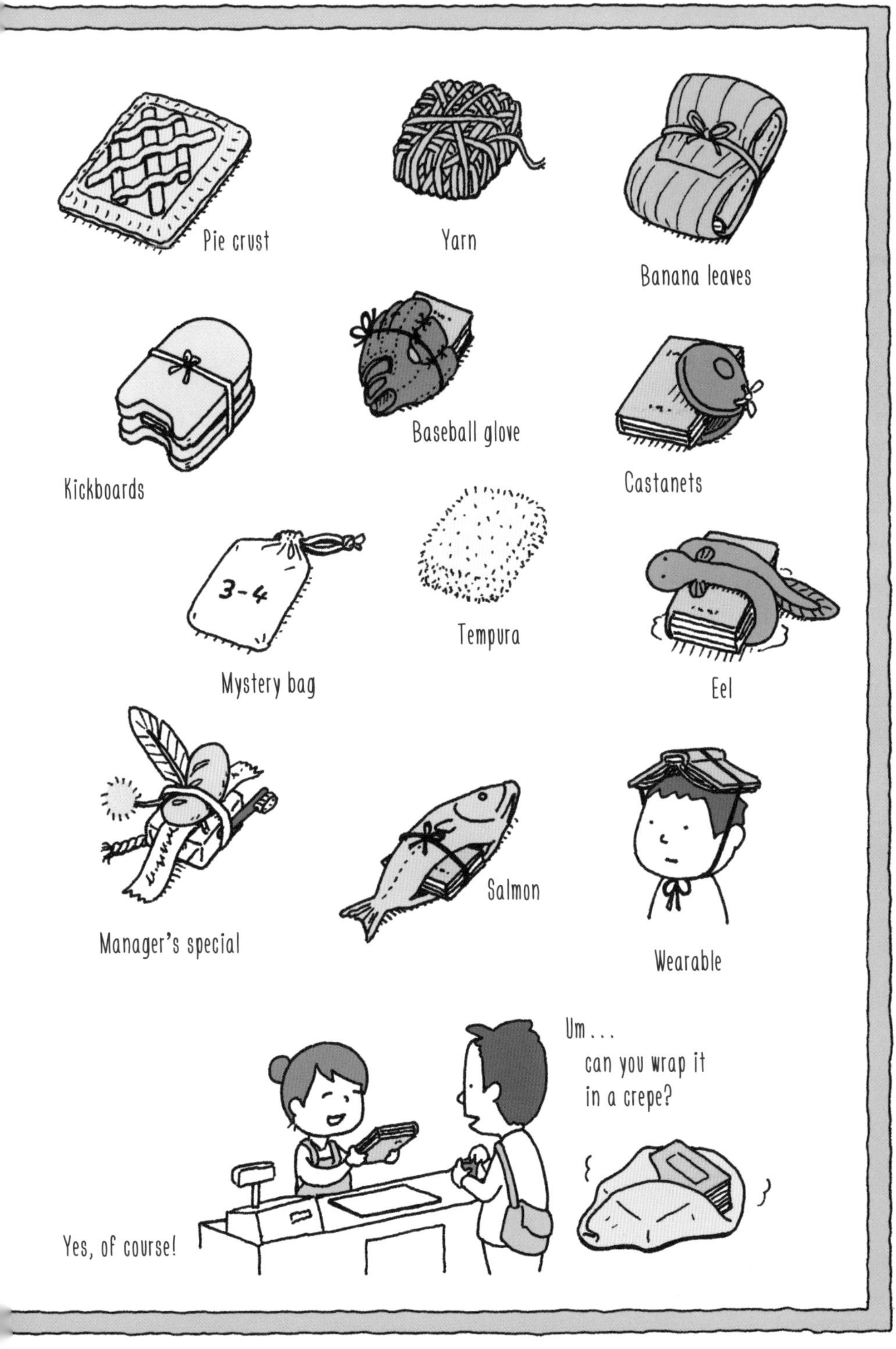

Pie crust
Yarn
Banana leaves
Kickboards
Baseball glove
Castanets
3-4
Mystery bag
Tempura
Eel
Manager's special
Salmon
Wearable
Um . . .
can you wrap it
in a crepe?
Yes, of course!

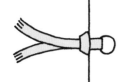

"PAPERBACK DOGS"

1. Paperback dogs first accompanied rescue dogs and provided an interesting book to entertain people in distress while they waited for the rescue team.

2. Nowadays, the main duty of paperback dogs is to seek out people who are isolated from society or live alone and provide them with some light, entertaining reading.

3. The most intuitive paperback dogs are able to study a person in need, identify an appropriate genre, and take such a book to them.

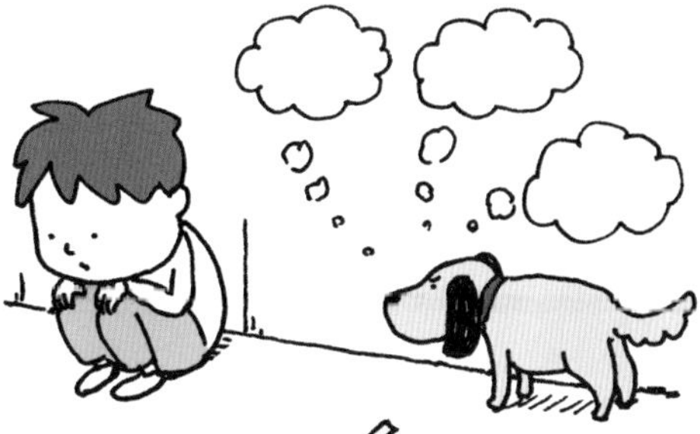

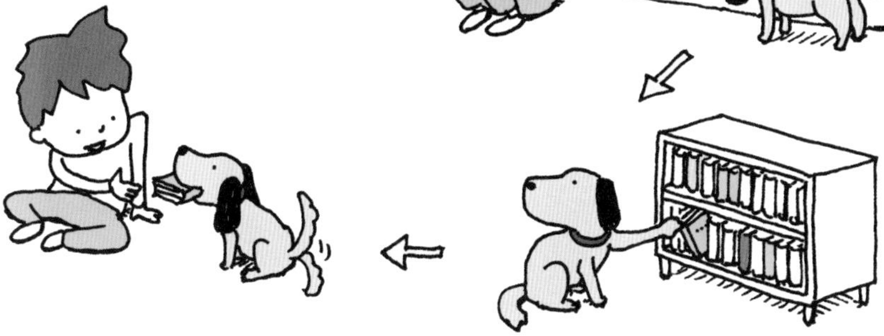

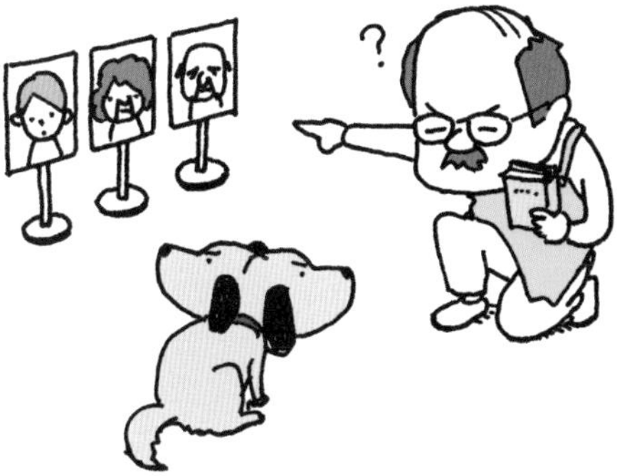
?

4. A wide range of knowledge and skill is required to train a paperback dog to do this. Trainers are usually dog-loving, retired bookstore managers.

5. In earlier times, in addition to paperback dogs, paperback pigeons would deliver books to people living in remote regions.

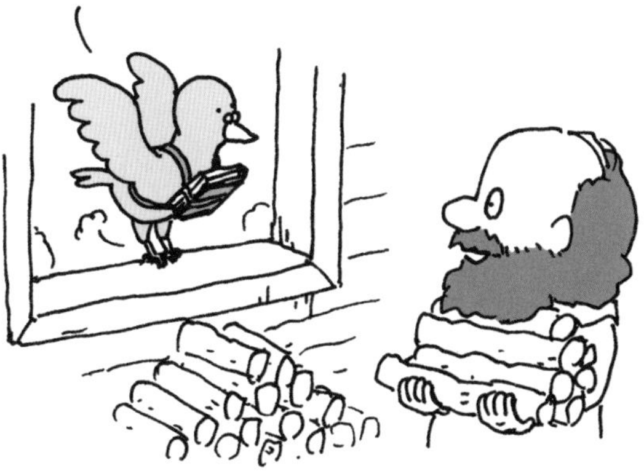

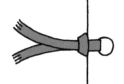

"BOOK COLLECTION ARCHIVE SPECIALISTS"

...You have a wonderful book collection!

I worry though that these books will not live up to their full potential hidden away like this.

Who are you?

I'm sorry. Allow me to introduce myself. I am from the Association for Archiving Brilliant Book Collections.

We would like to preserve this entire bookcase in optimal environmental conditions so that we can forever archive your impeccable taste in these fascinating volumes.

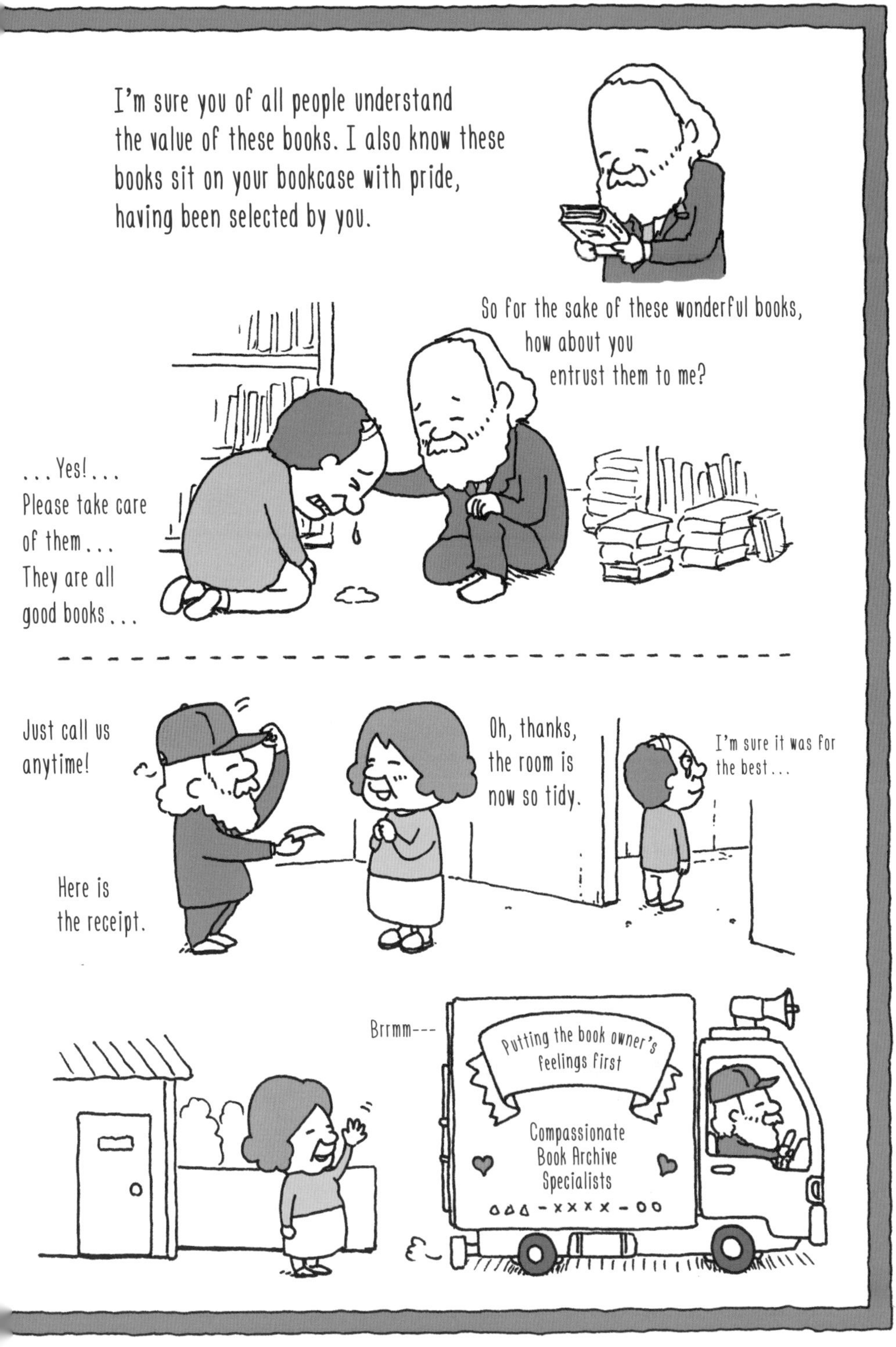
I'm sure you of all people understand the value of these books. I also know these books sit on your bookcase with pride, having been selected by you.
So for the sake of these wonderful books, how about you entrust them to me?
...Yes!... Please take care of them... They are all good books...
Just call us anytime!
Here is the receipt.
Oh, thanks, the room is now so tidy.
I'm sure it was for the best...
Brrmm---
Putting the book owner's feelings first
Compassionate Book Archive Specialists
△△△-××××-○○

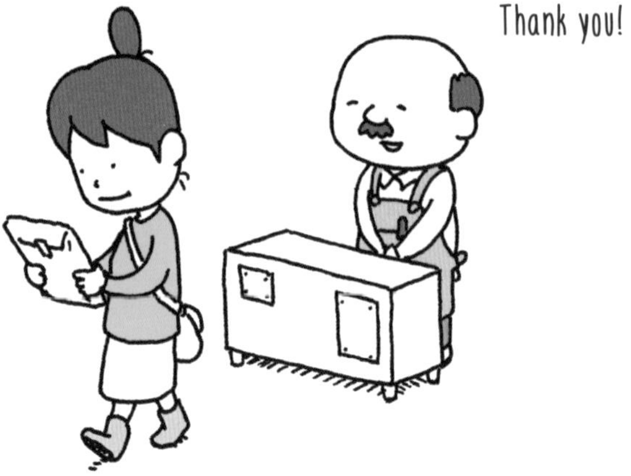
Thank you!

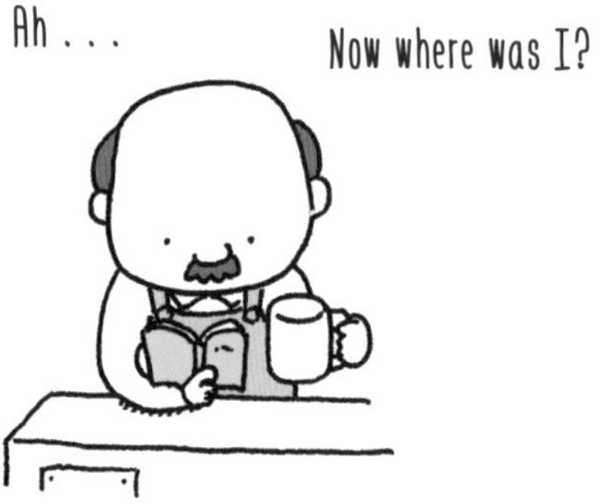
Ah . . .
Now where was I?

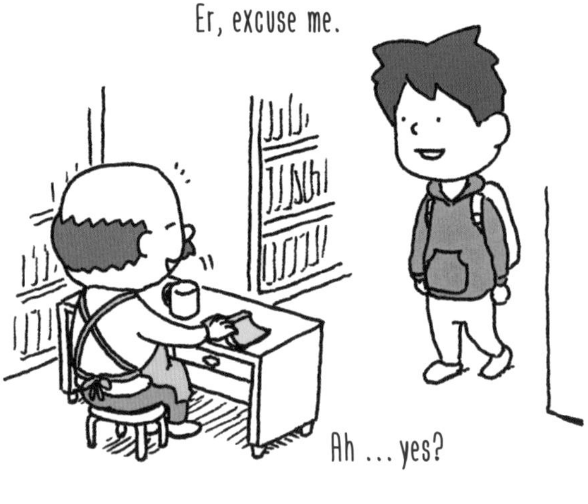
Er, excuse me.
Ah ... yes?

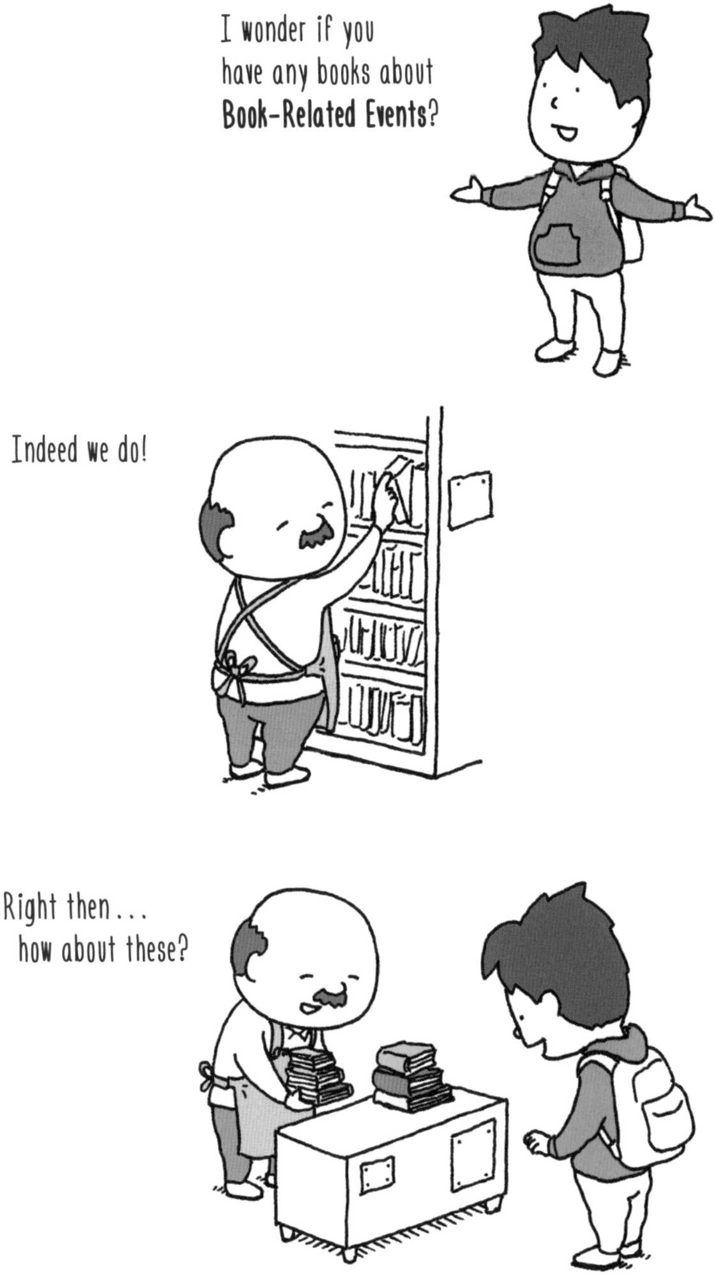
I wonder if you
have any books about
Book-Related Events?
Indeed we do!
Right then . . .
how about these?

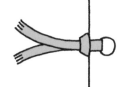

"UNIQUE BOOK FESTIVALS"

The Used-Book Parade

In this annual festival, used bookstores creat[e] bookcase floats and parade them down the street. The[y] compete for the best bookcase float as well as for th[e] finest book selection. Popular vote decides the winners[.]

The Spring Chase

In this festival, middle school students race to grab the only, early release copy of the next book in the thrilling Dragon Adventures book series.

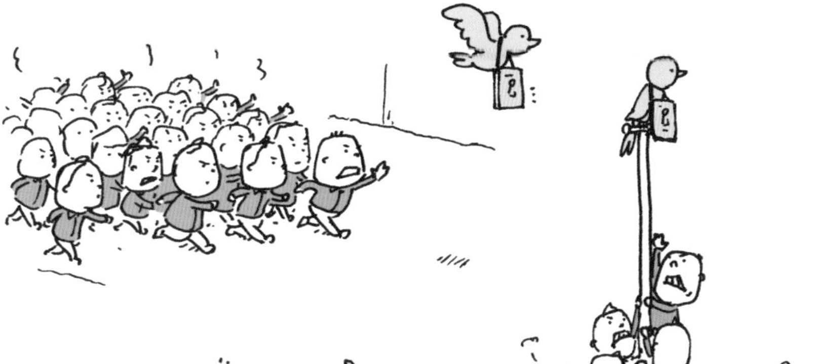

The student who gets hold of the book is granted the privilege of taking it home and reading it before anyone else.

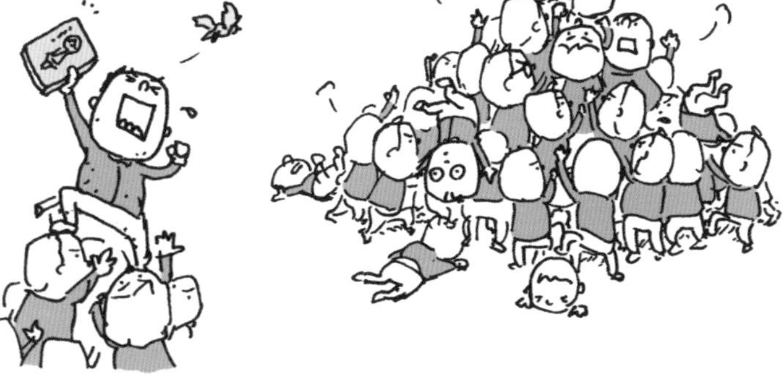

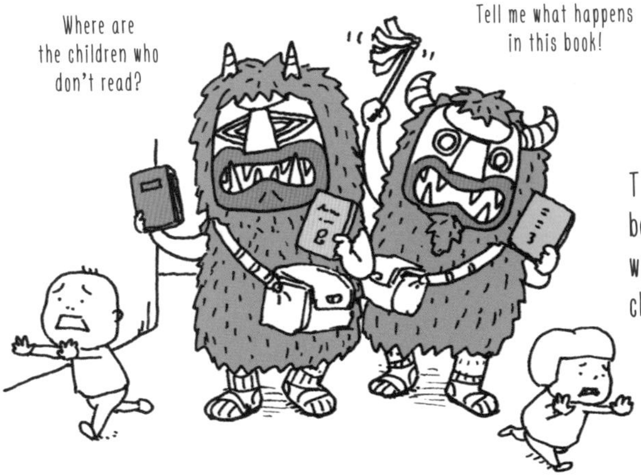
Where are the children who don't read?
Tell me what happens in this book!

The Reading Demon Festival

This festival is rumored to have been started by a PTA chairperson who worried about today's children not reading books.

Every year there is lively debate as to its effectiveness.

"A BOOKSTORE WEDDING"

1. The marriage of a book-loving couple is celebrated at a bookstore.

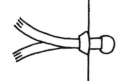

The wedding gifts are book vouchers.

2. The newlyweds arrive.

3. The couple's entire reading history is presented.

4. The time they met is re-created.

5. During the family speeches, guests may read their favorite books.

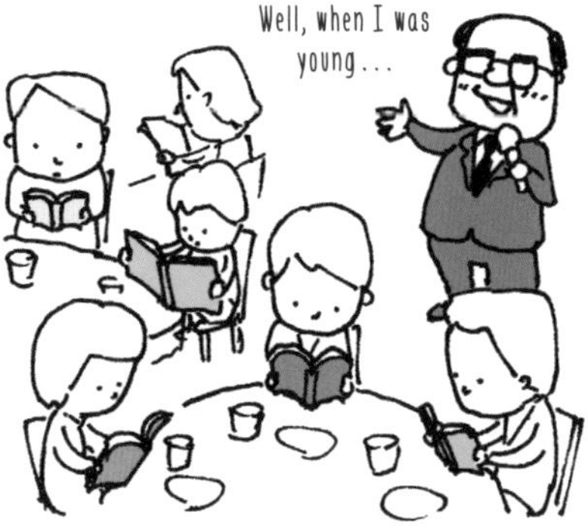
Well, when I was young...

6. The inserting of the bookmark.

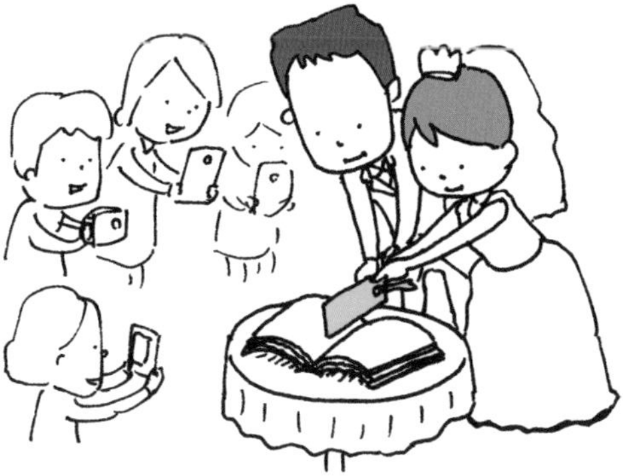

7. Bride recites beautiful poems to her future in-laws.

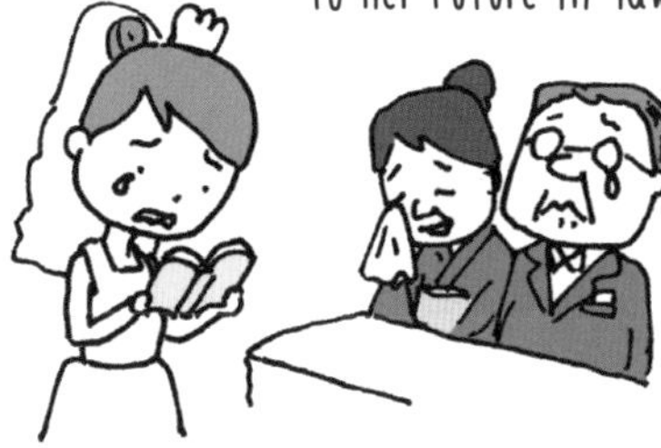

8. Tossing the paperback...

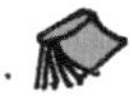

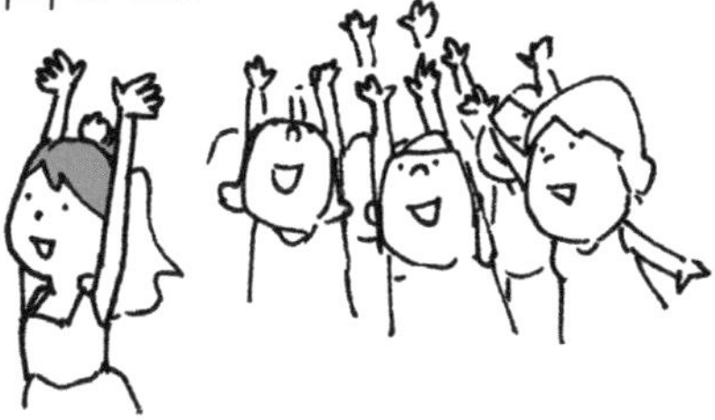

9. Reading of vows by the bookstore manager.

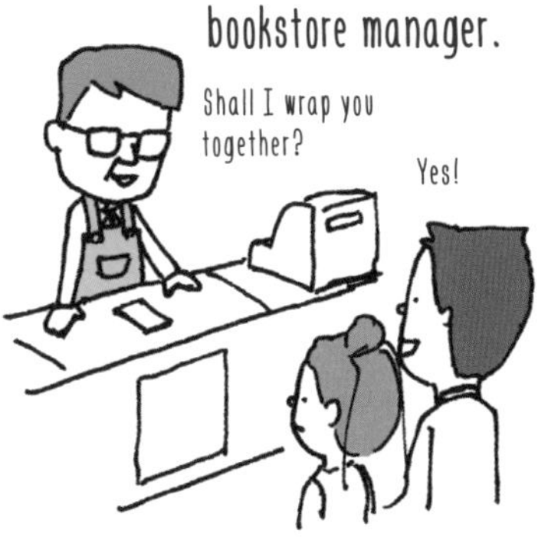
Shall I wrap you together?
Yes!

10. Newlyweds leave.

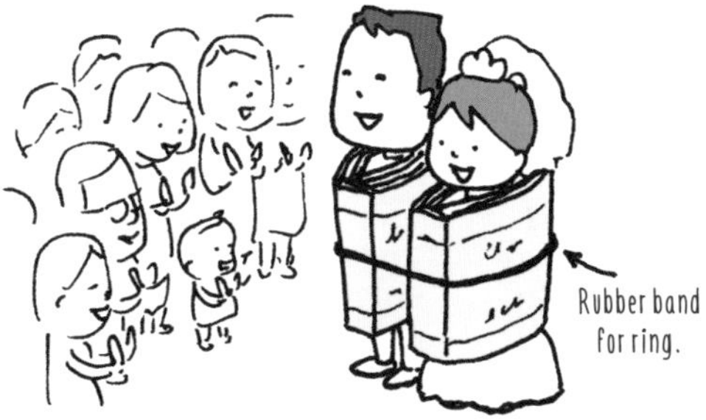
Rubber band for ring.

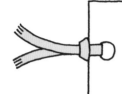

"THE POWER OF IMAGINATION BOOK-WRITING RELAY"

1. At a used bookstore, buy an intriguing book written who knows when, in an unknown language saying who knows what.

2. Show the book to various people and ask, "What do you think this book is about?" Listen to what they imagine.

3. Ask them to channel their creative energies and write summaries of the book.

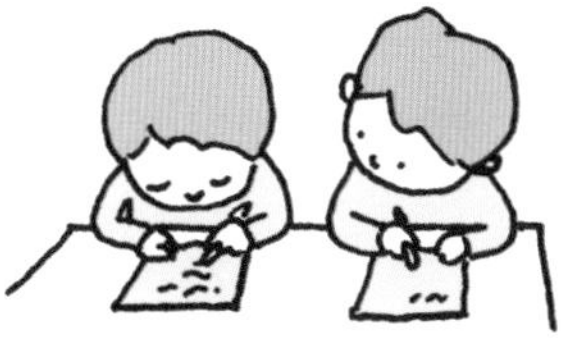

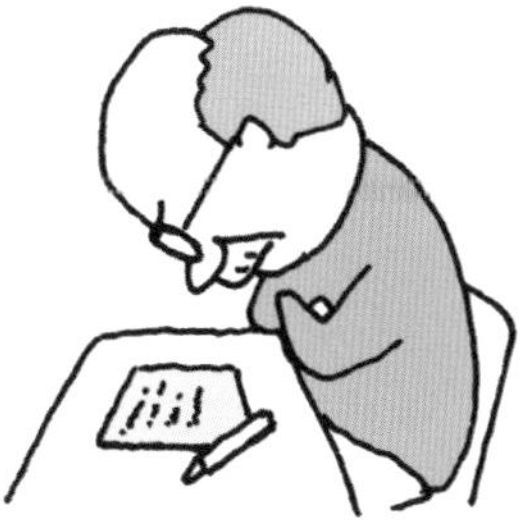

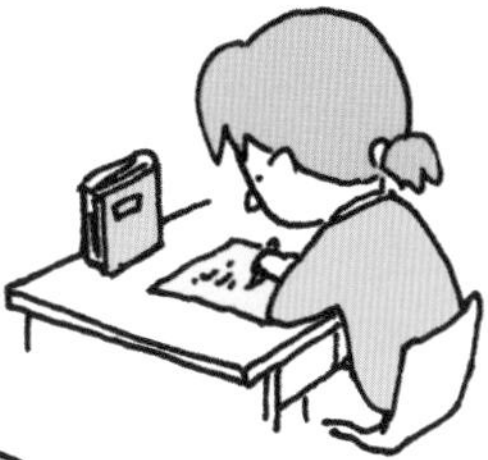

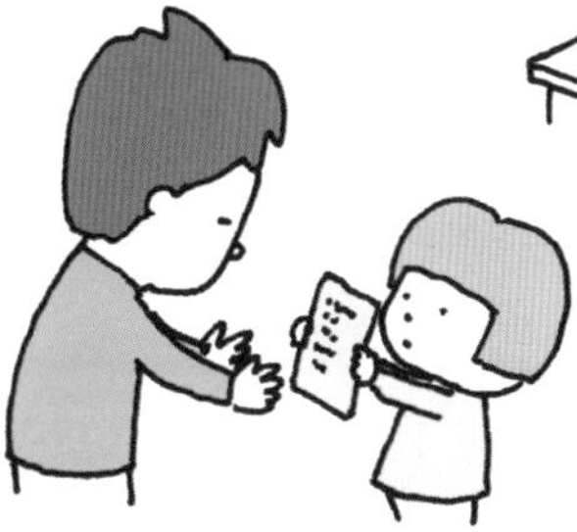

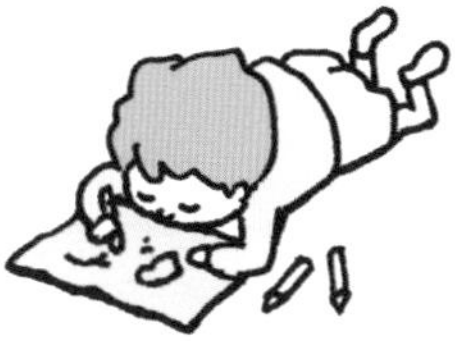

4. Compile all these summaries together, and translate them into your own made-up language that says who knows what, and bind them into a single book.

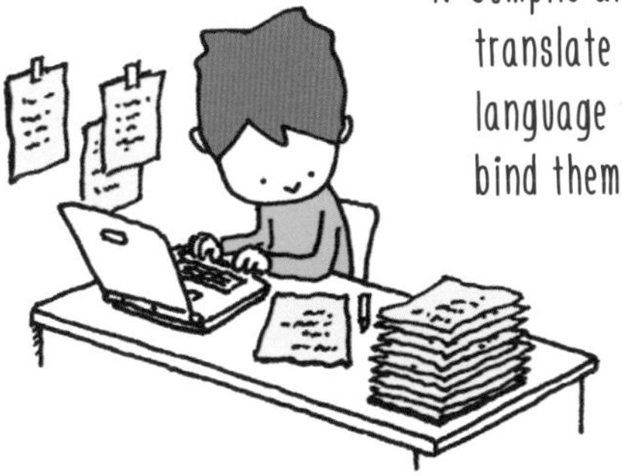

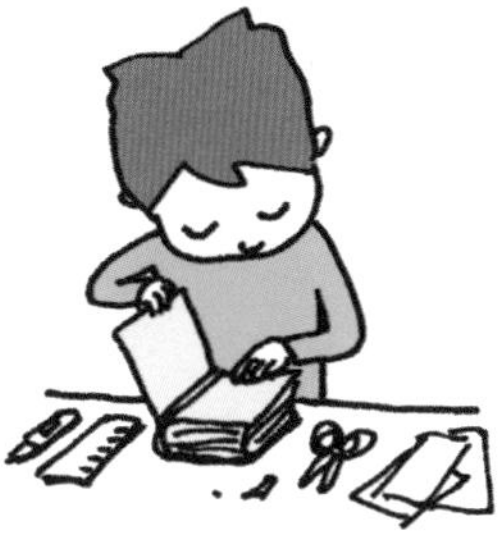

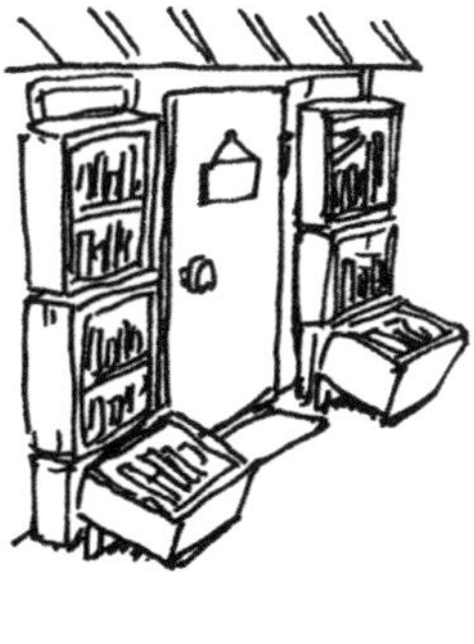

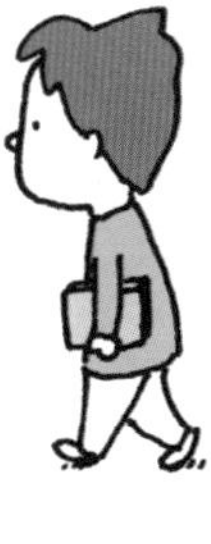

5. Go and sell that book to a used bookstore.

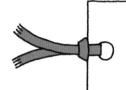

"AN AROUND-THE-WORLD READING TRIP"

Take a trip around the world while leisurely reading inside a special capsule.

You can enjoy reading while taking in amazing scenery.

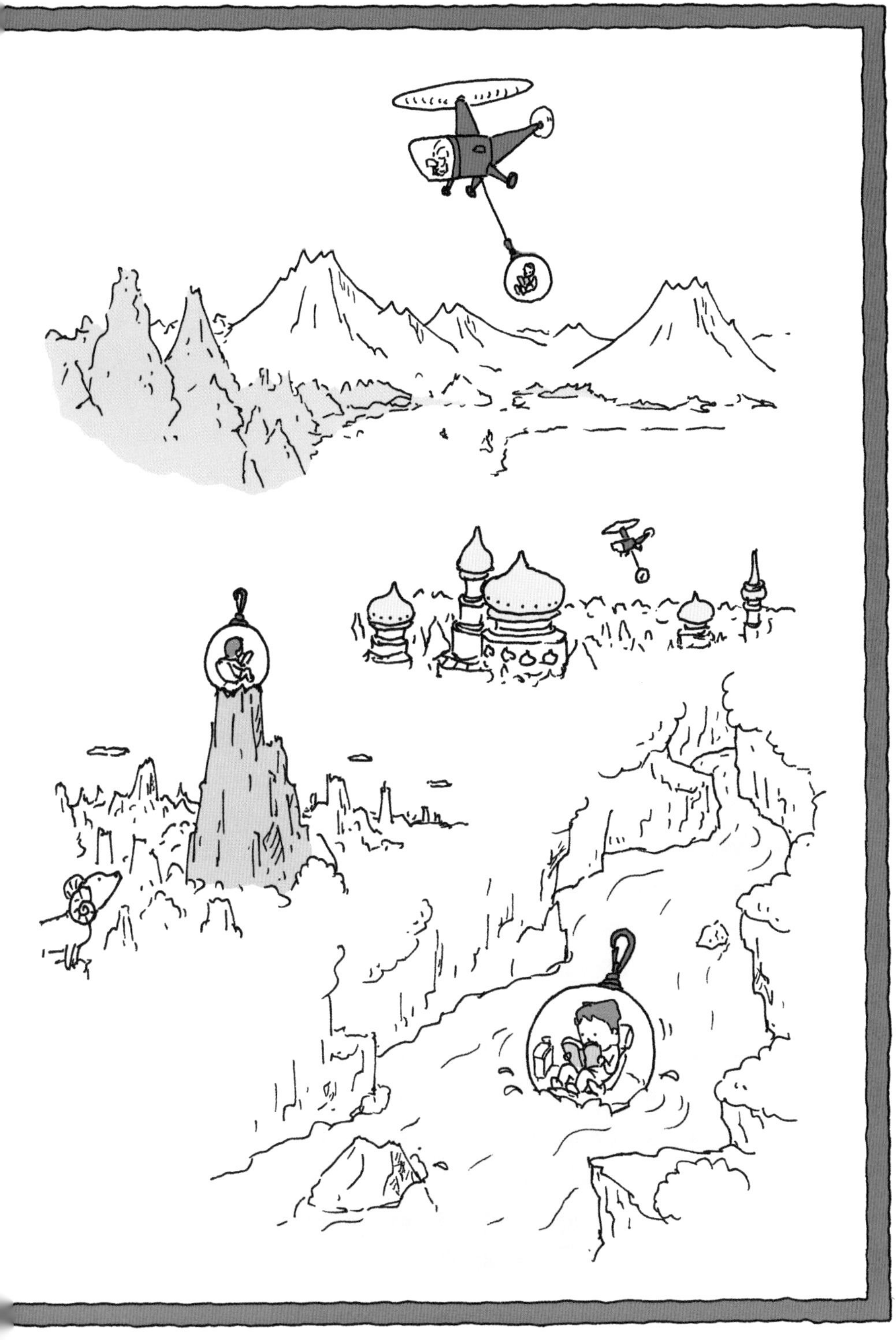

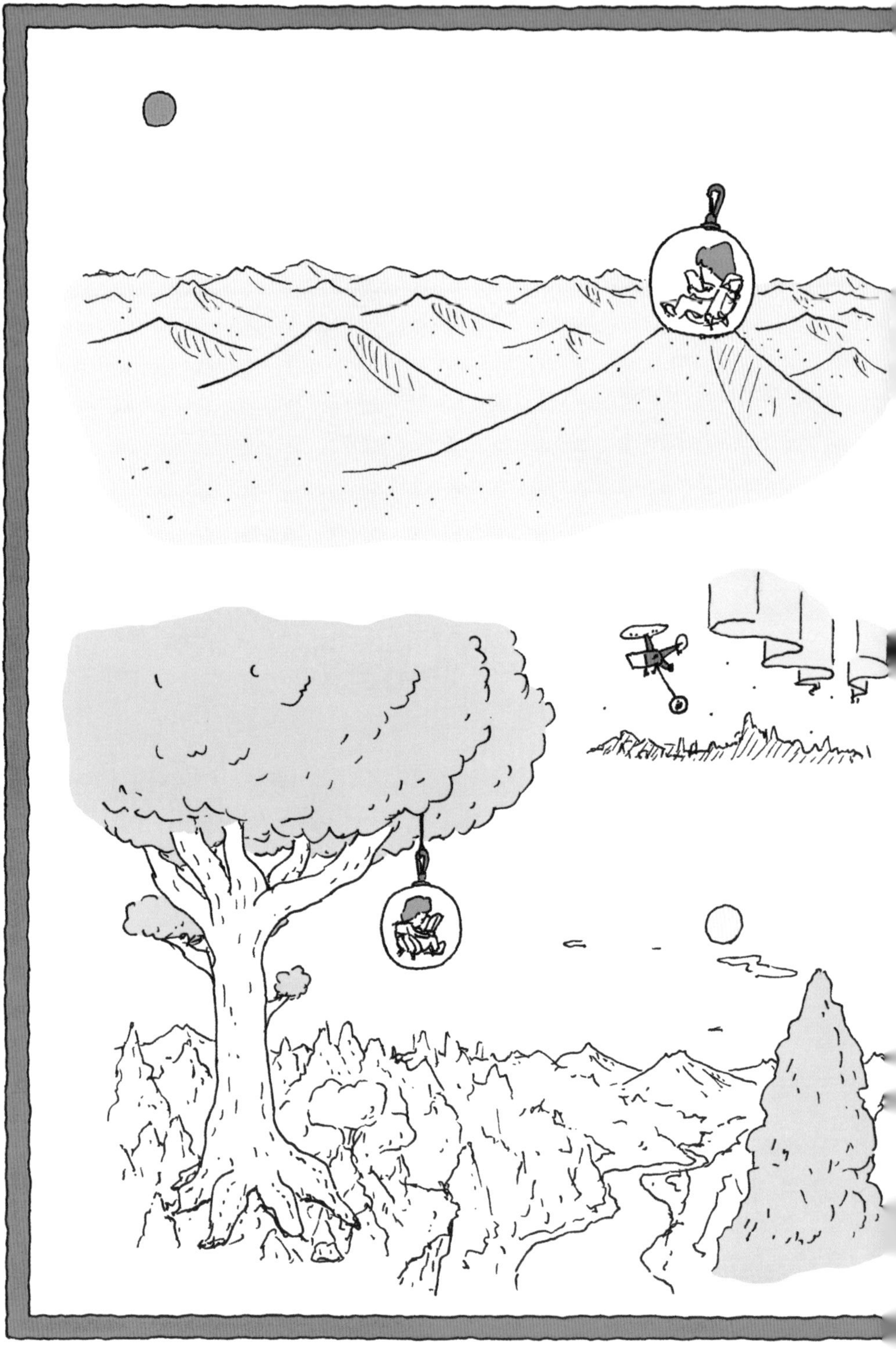

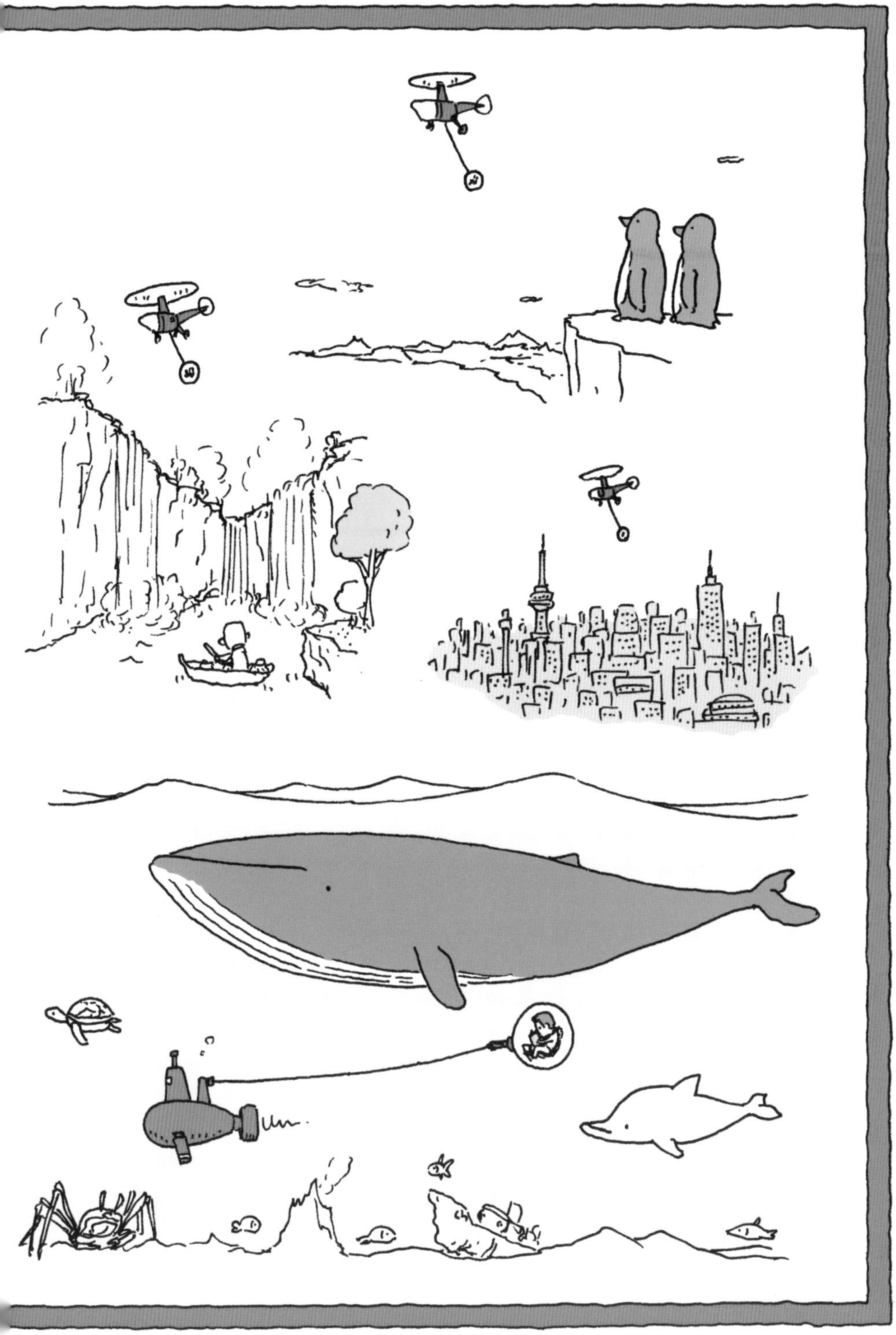

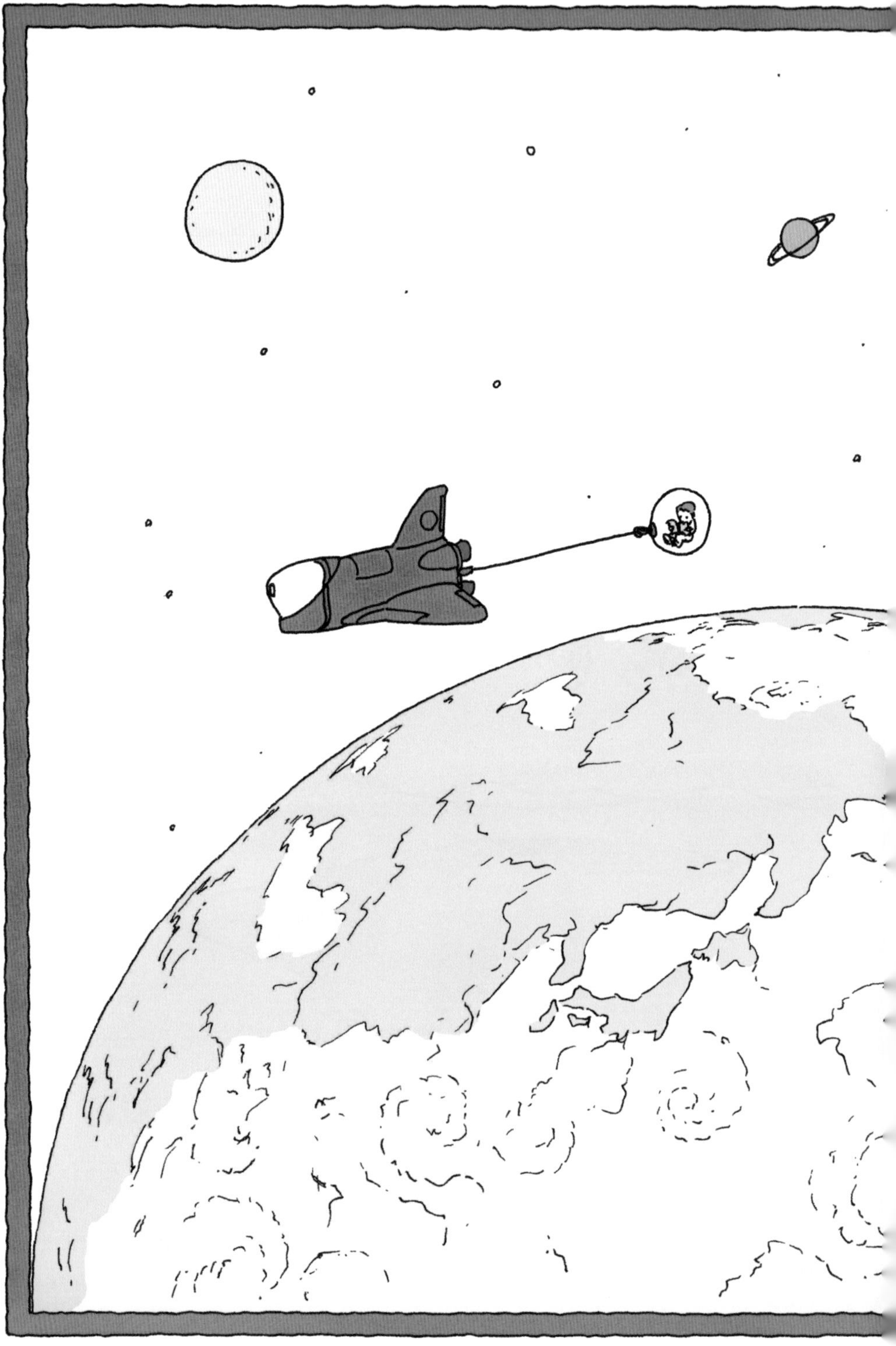

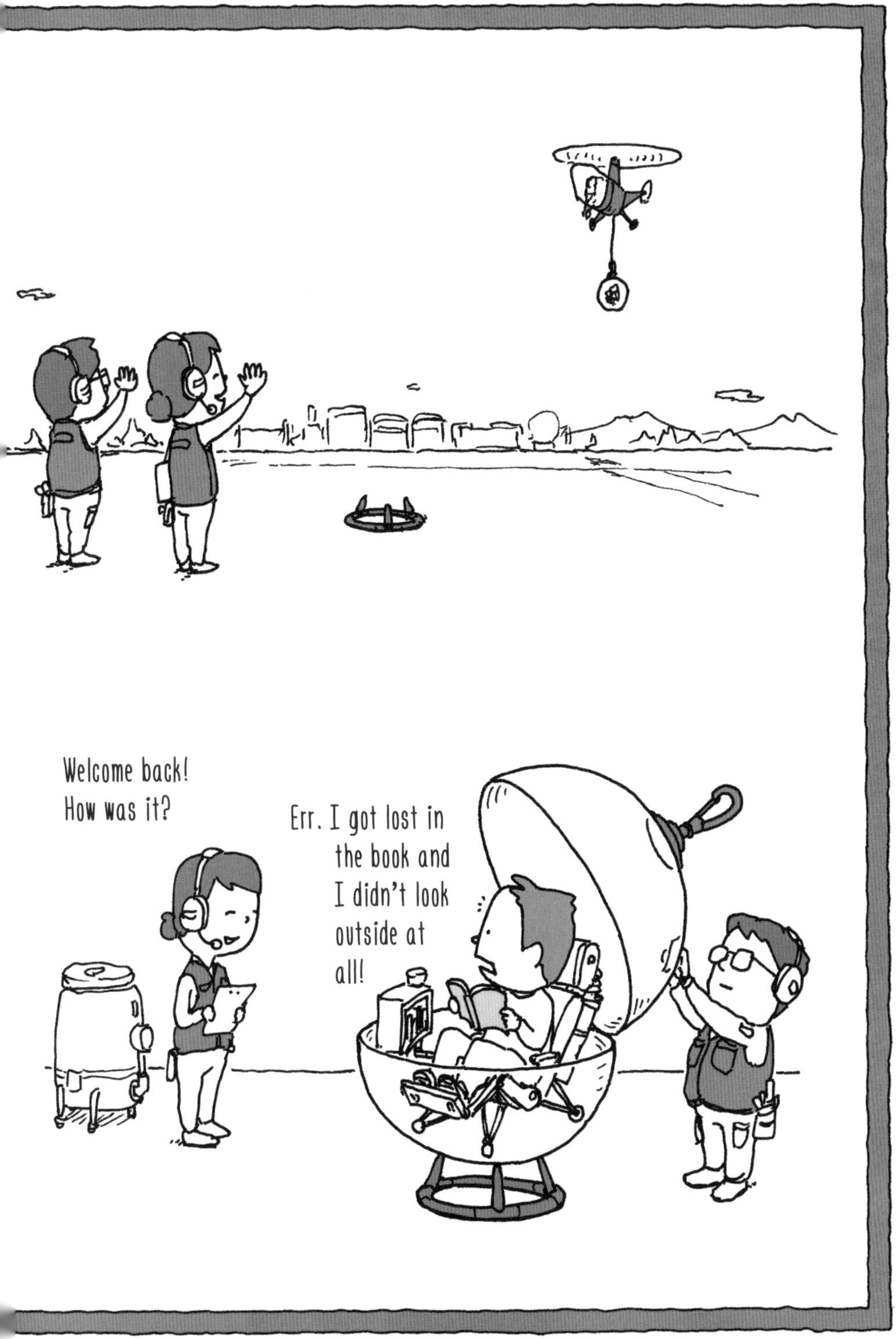
Welcome back!
How was it?
Err. I got lost in the book and I didn't look outside at all!

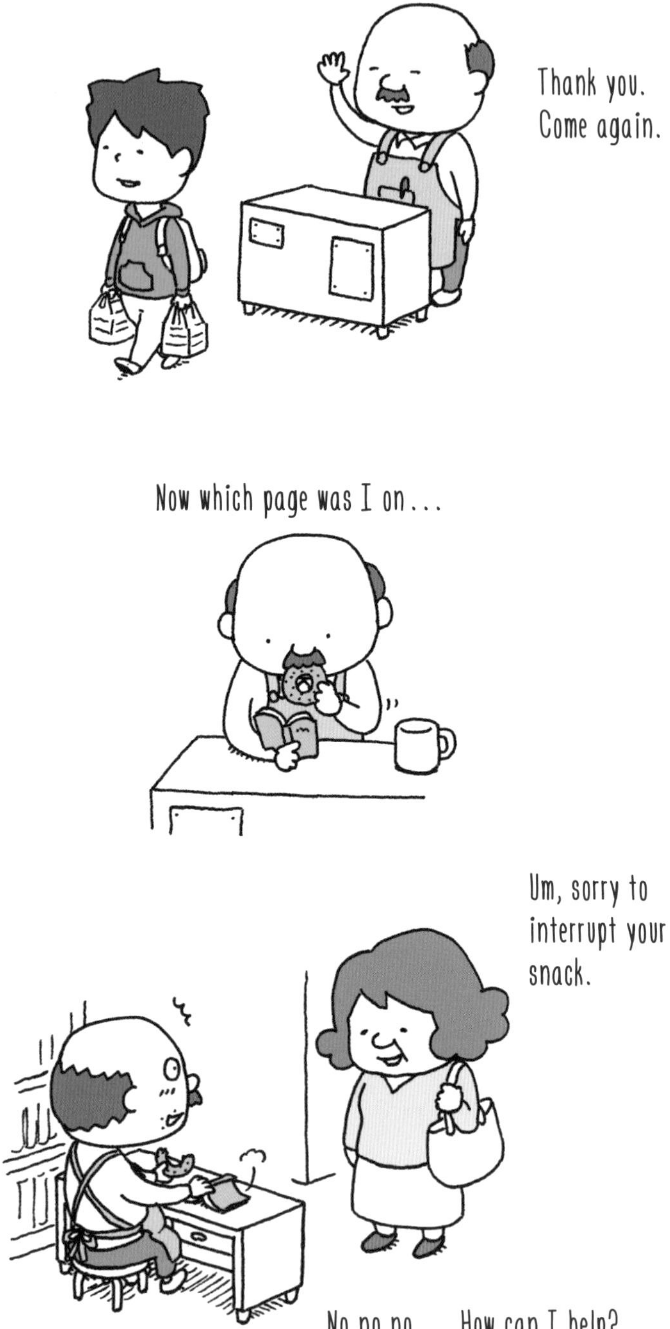
Thank you.
Come again.
Now which page was I on...
Um, sorry to
interrupt your
snack.
No no no... How can I help?

I wonder if you have any books on **Famous Book-Related Places?**

Yes, we certainly do.

Here you are. See if there is anything you like out of these.

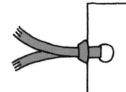

"THE VILLAGE OF RAINING BOOKS"

1. When the rainy season comes around in this particular area, books start falling from the sky.

2. The books quickly start piling up, so unless you begin shoveling early...

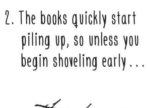

3. .... you won't be able to leave the house.

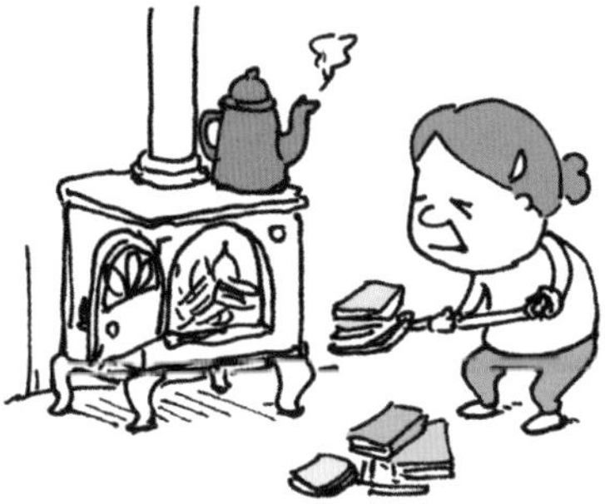

4. The excess books can be used for fuel, or even as building material for houses.

But mostly, they are taken to the cliff at the edge of the village . . .

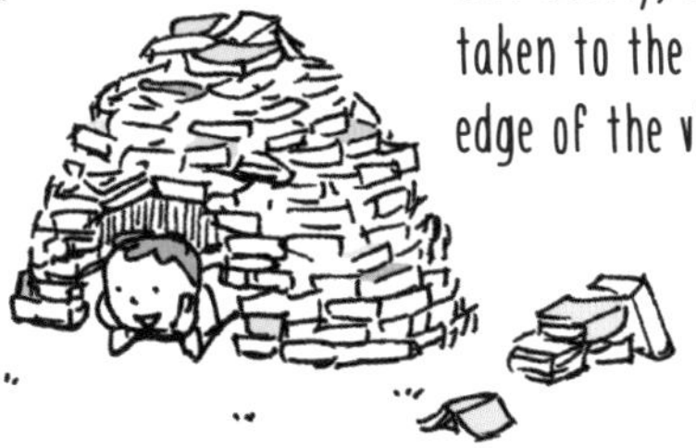

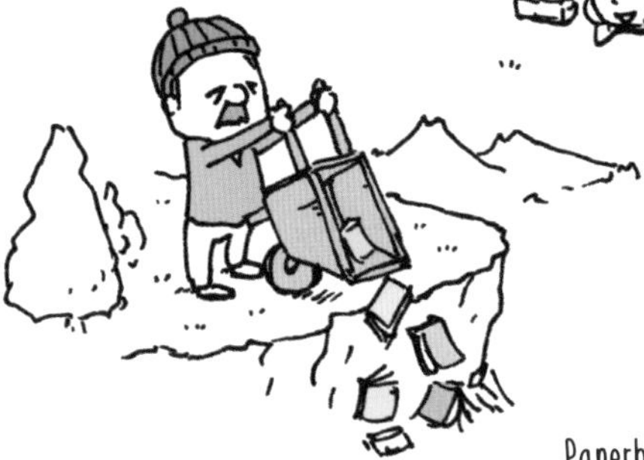

. . . and dumped.

5. At the bottom of the cliff, the books that have fallen down over the years have created literary strata.

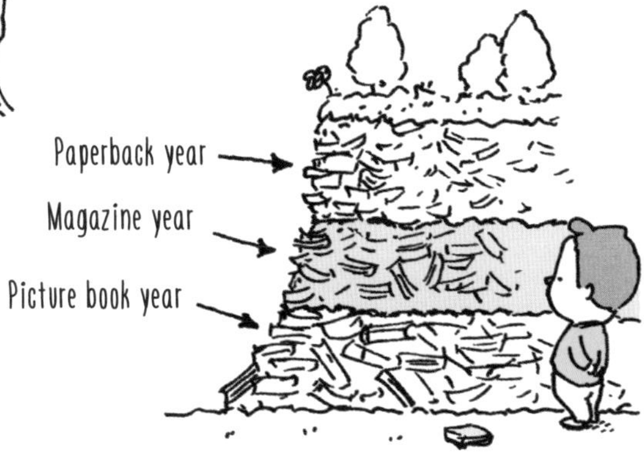
Paperback year
Magazine year
Picture book year

6. People come from afar to feast their eyes on all the books there to be freely read.

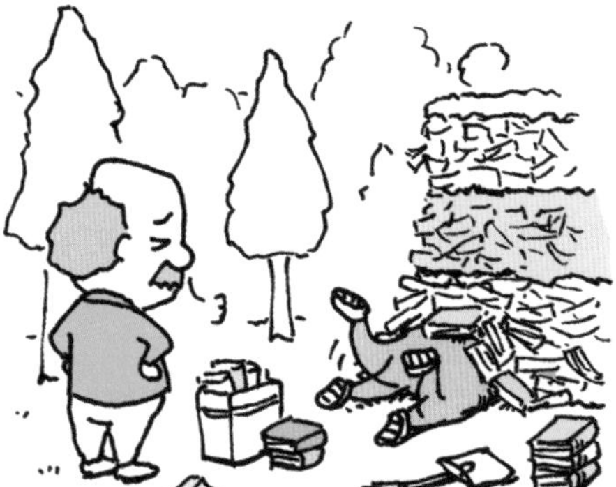

Each year, though, a few people become trapped under the layers and need to be rescued.

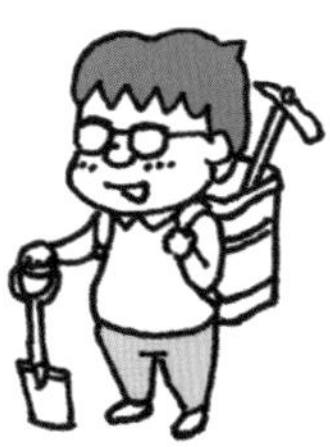

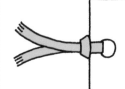

"THE READING REED"

1. Once every five years, in a very special place, a reading phenomenon occurs during which all living creatures start reading.

2. The event coincides with the once-every-five-years flowering of the Reading Reed, which only grows in this location. Scientists have studied the plant to determine if something in the pollen or scent of this flower could be the cause.

3. Once the flowers wilt, however, a counter-phenomenon of reading fatigue sets in, lasting for about two months.

4. When this happens, the scientists studying the plant no longer want to read, and their research remains unfinished. How the plant produces these effects remains unknown even today.

By the Water's Edge
Book Signing
by Professor Estuary

5. Naturally, each creature has its own favorite type of book.

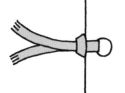

"THE TOMBSTONE BOOKCASE"

1. The tombstone bookcase is a way of sharing books with someone after they have passed away.

2. Inside are various books: those that the deceased had loved, those that made an impact on his or her life, and those that the deceased wanted dear ones to read someday.

3. The visitor selects one book and places it in a bag.

4. Then the visitor places a new book that he or she recommends into the bookcase so that the deceased may read it in heaven.

5. The visitor closes the door and thinks fondly of the deceased.

6. The visitor then heads home, looking forward to reading the book in the bag.

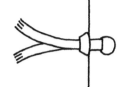

"THE UNDERWATER LIBRARY"

Once upon a time there was a rich man.

He dearly loved books.

In his final days, he built a very tall library at the bottom of a deep hollow.

He filled the library with his personal collection of books, old and new, from far and wide.

From bottom to top—nothing but books.

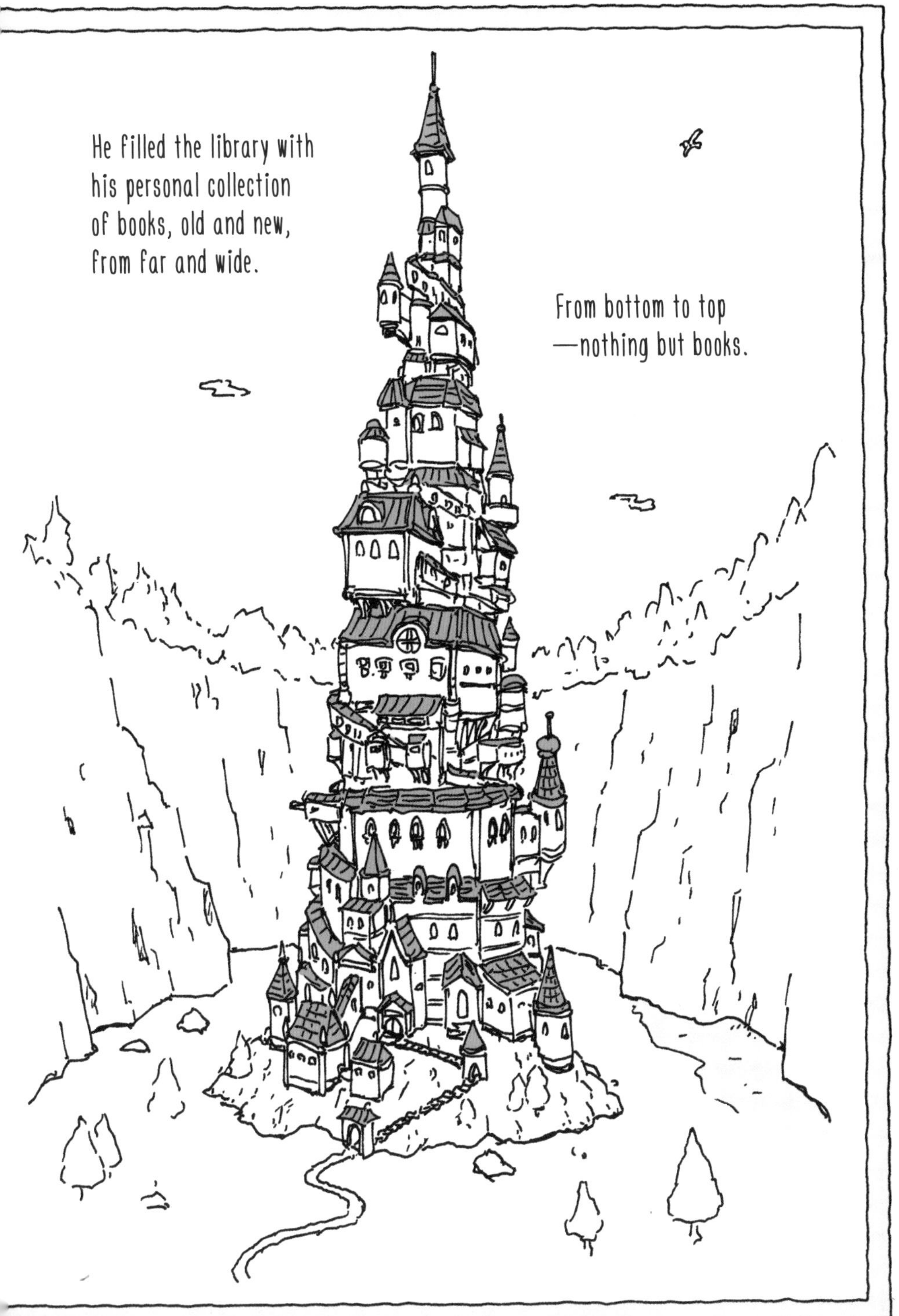

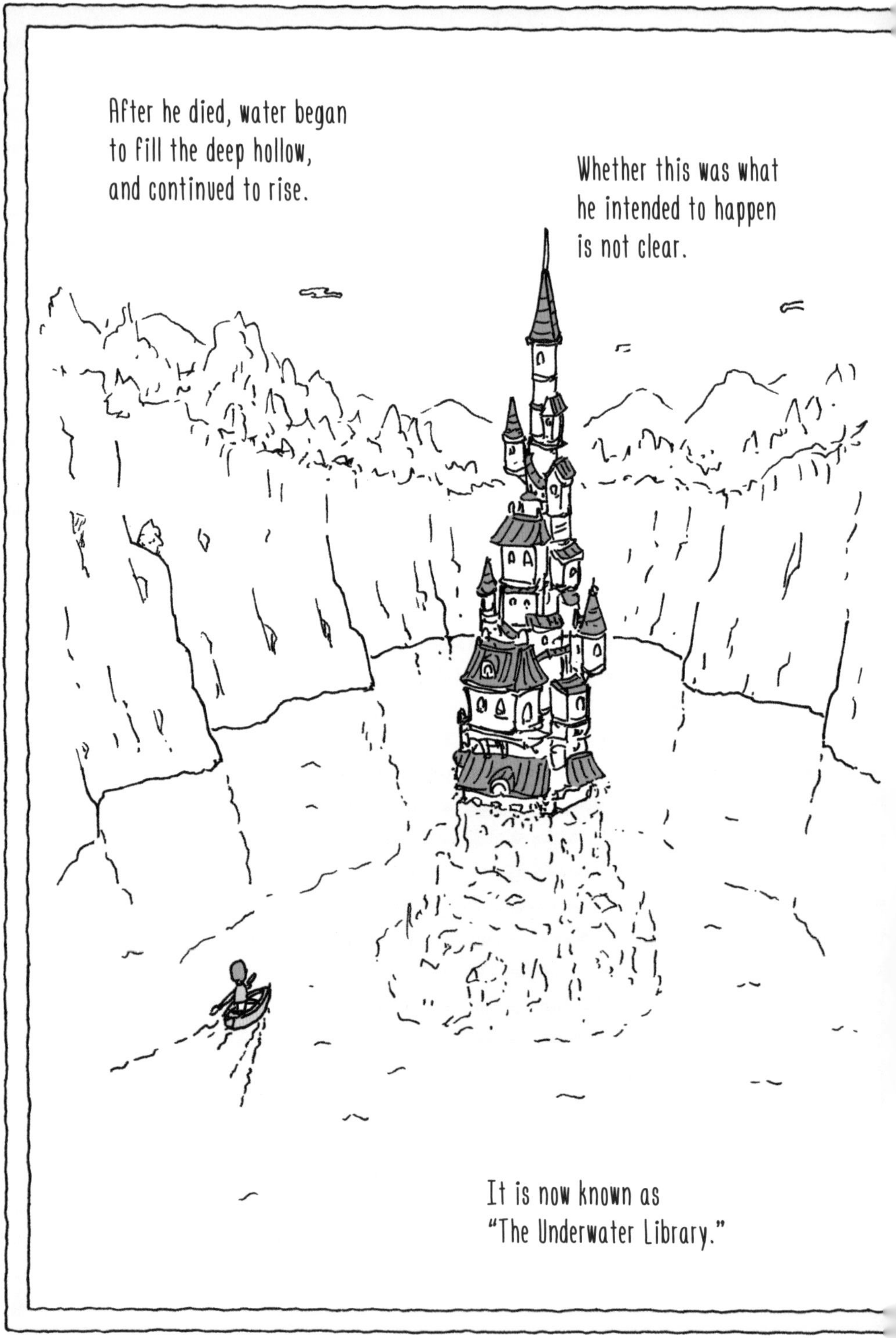
After he died, water began to fill the deep hollow, and continued to rise.
Whether this was what he intended to happen is not clear.
It is now known as "The Underwater Library."

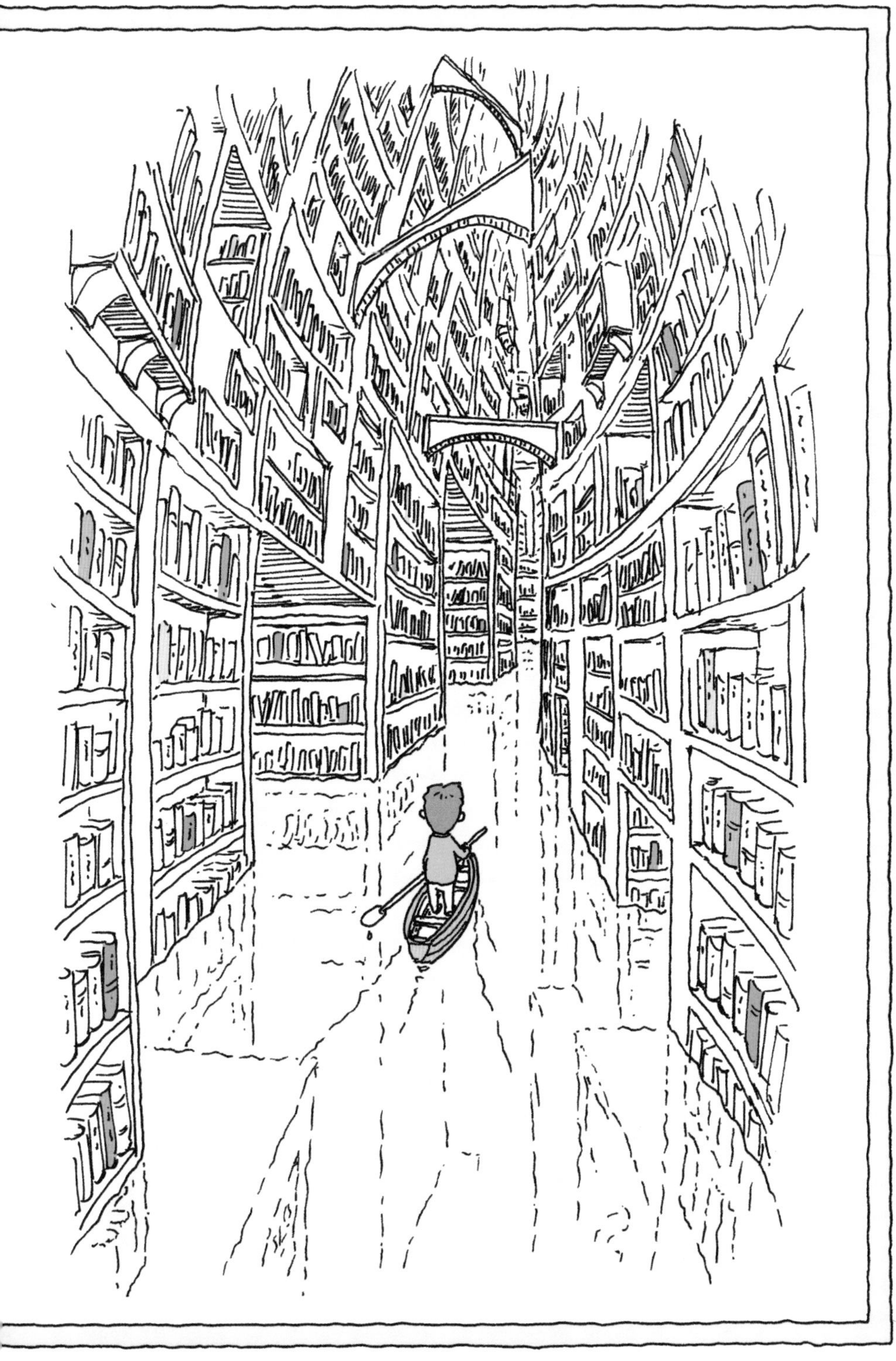

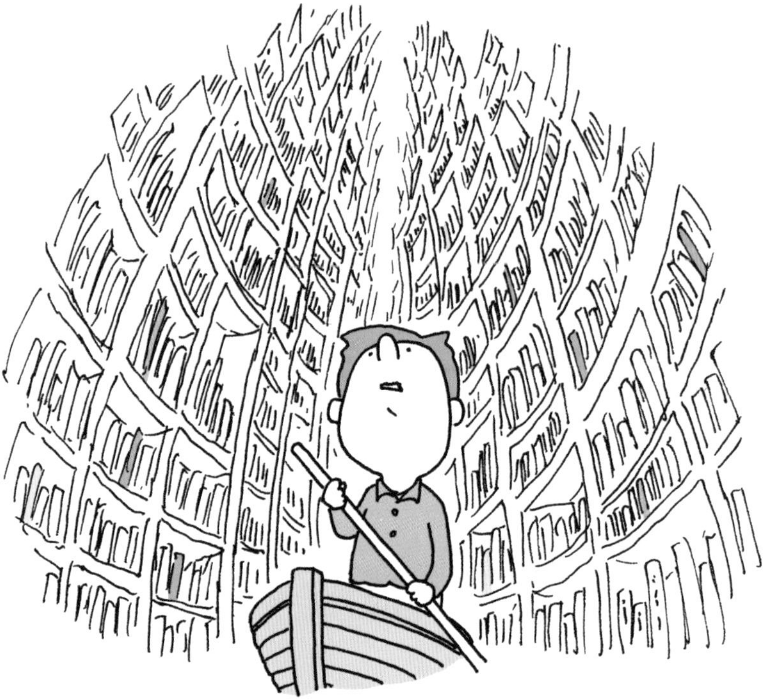

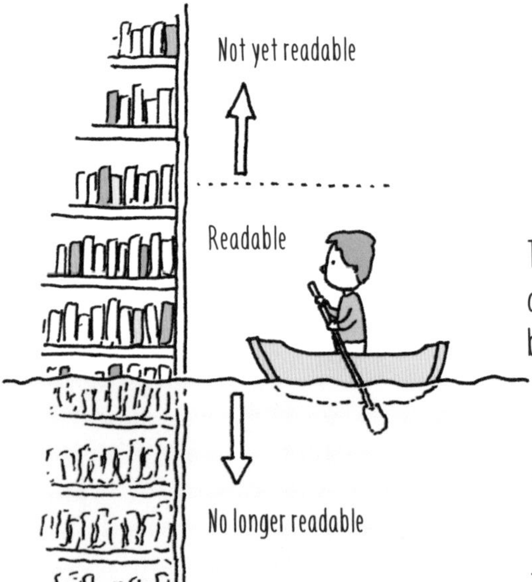
Not yet readable
Readable
No longer readable

The books on the shelves already under the water are unreadable.

The books on the shelves up above are unreachable, and cannot be read . . . yet.

Every year, the water level rises. One day, it will be possible to read the books on even the highest shelves.

What books are on the topmost shelf?

Locals speculate about this from time to time.

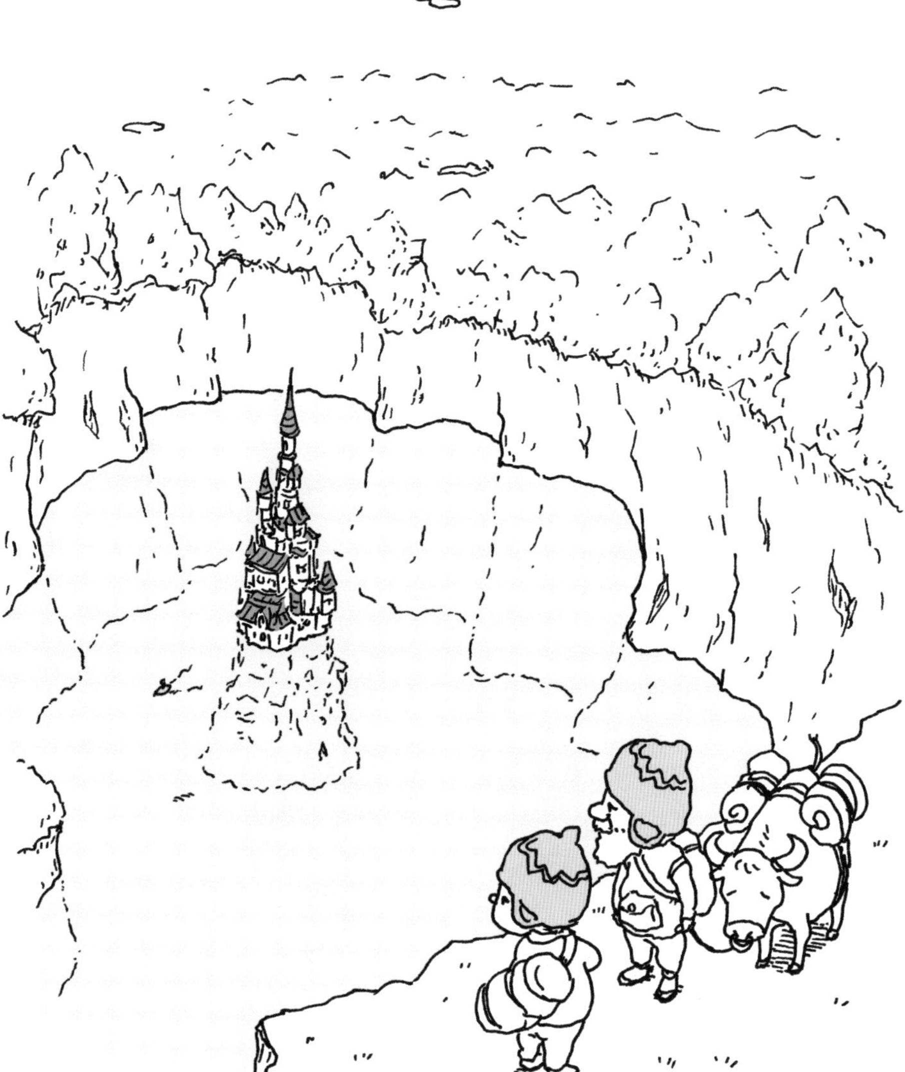

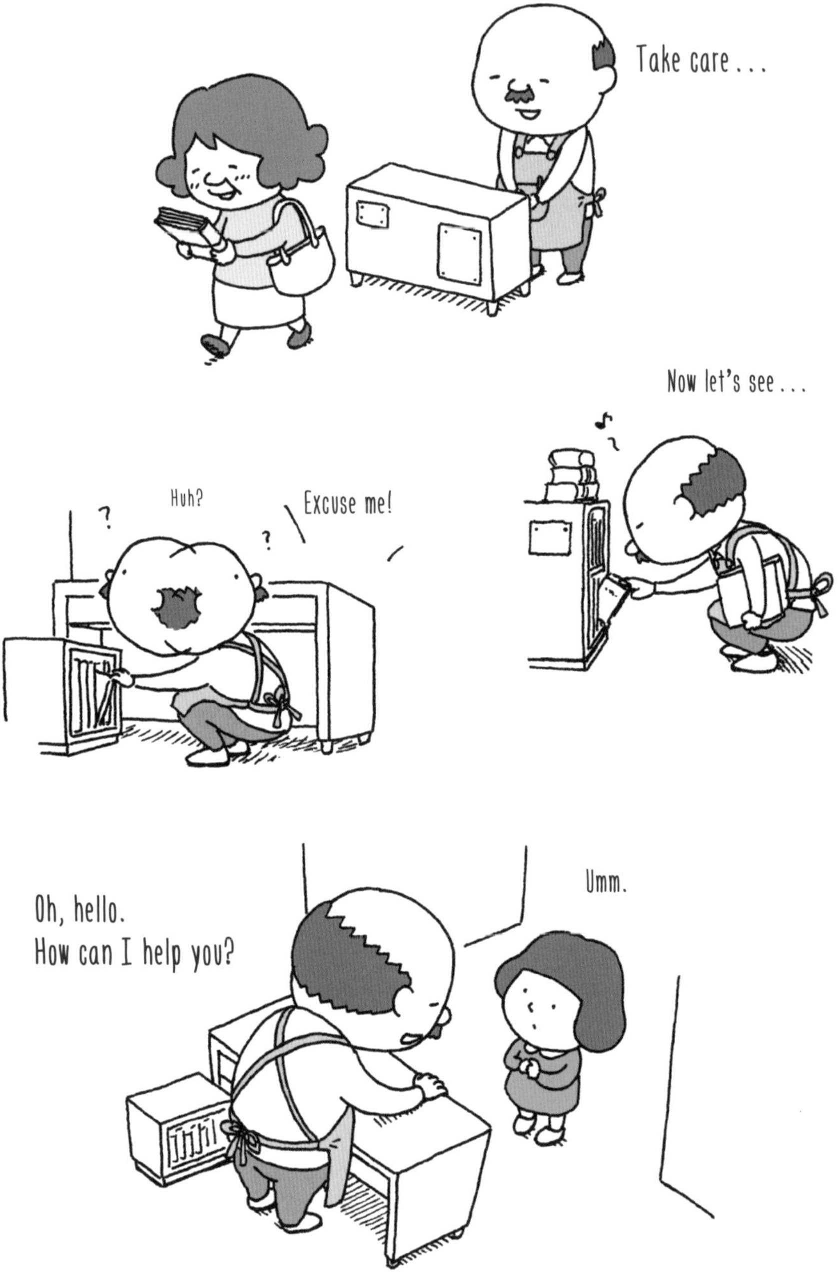
Take care...
Now let's see...
Huh?
Excuse me!
Oh, hello.
How can I help you?
Umm.

I wonder if you have any books about **The Book Itself**?

Yes, sure thing!

Are these the sort of books you are looking for?

"WHY BOOKS ARE RECTANGULAR"

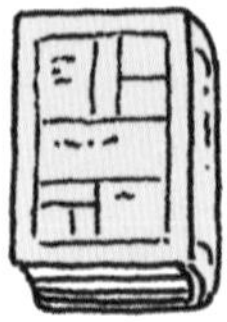

1. Once upon a time, books were made in all kinds of shapes.

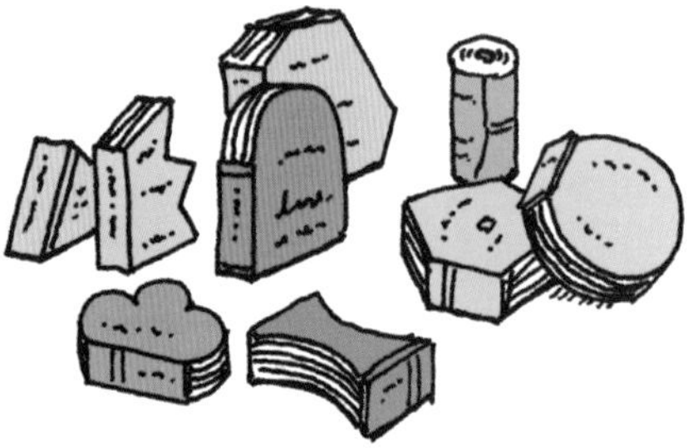

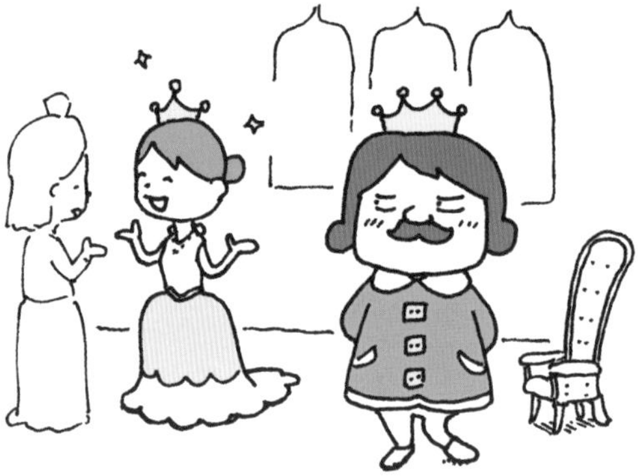

2. In those days, the king of a certain land really liked the princes of the neighboring kingdom.

But he was much too shy to talk to her.

3. At a party one day, the princess came up and spoke to the king for the first time.

"I love the rectangular buttons on your coat. They're so cute!"

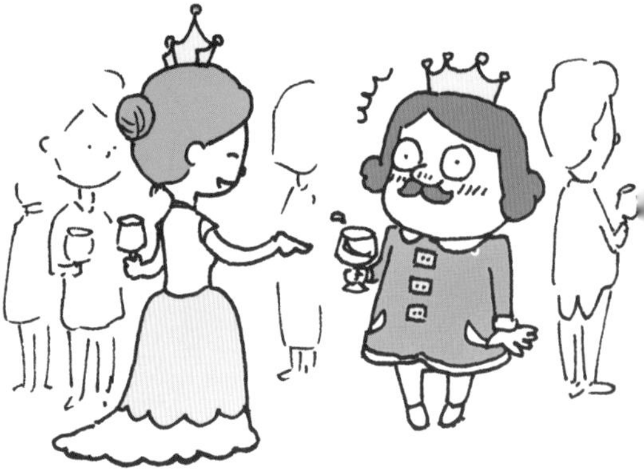

4. "Aha, she likes rectangular things!" the King thought. So he made everything about himself and his kingdom rectangular, hoping that the princess would like him.

5. Unfortunately, the princess ended up marrying the ruler of a different country.

   His face was a perfect circle.

6. As time passed and the rectangular kingdom expanded, its style of books spread and became popular around the world.

   "Why rectangular?" people would ask. The king would offer many different explanations, but would never reveal the real reason why.

"HOW TO MAKE BOOKS"

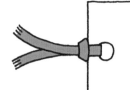

1. Combine the various ingredients—paper, text, photos, and illustrations—and slice the contents to the proper length as it extrudes from the mixer.

Text
Illustrations
Photos
Paper

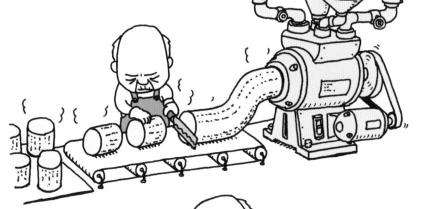

2. Begin shaving while rotating the book tube.

shik-shik-shik

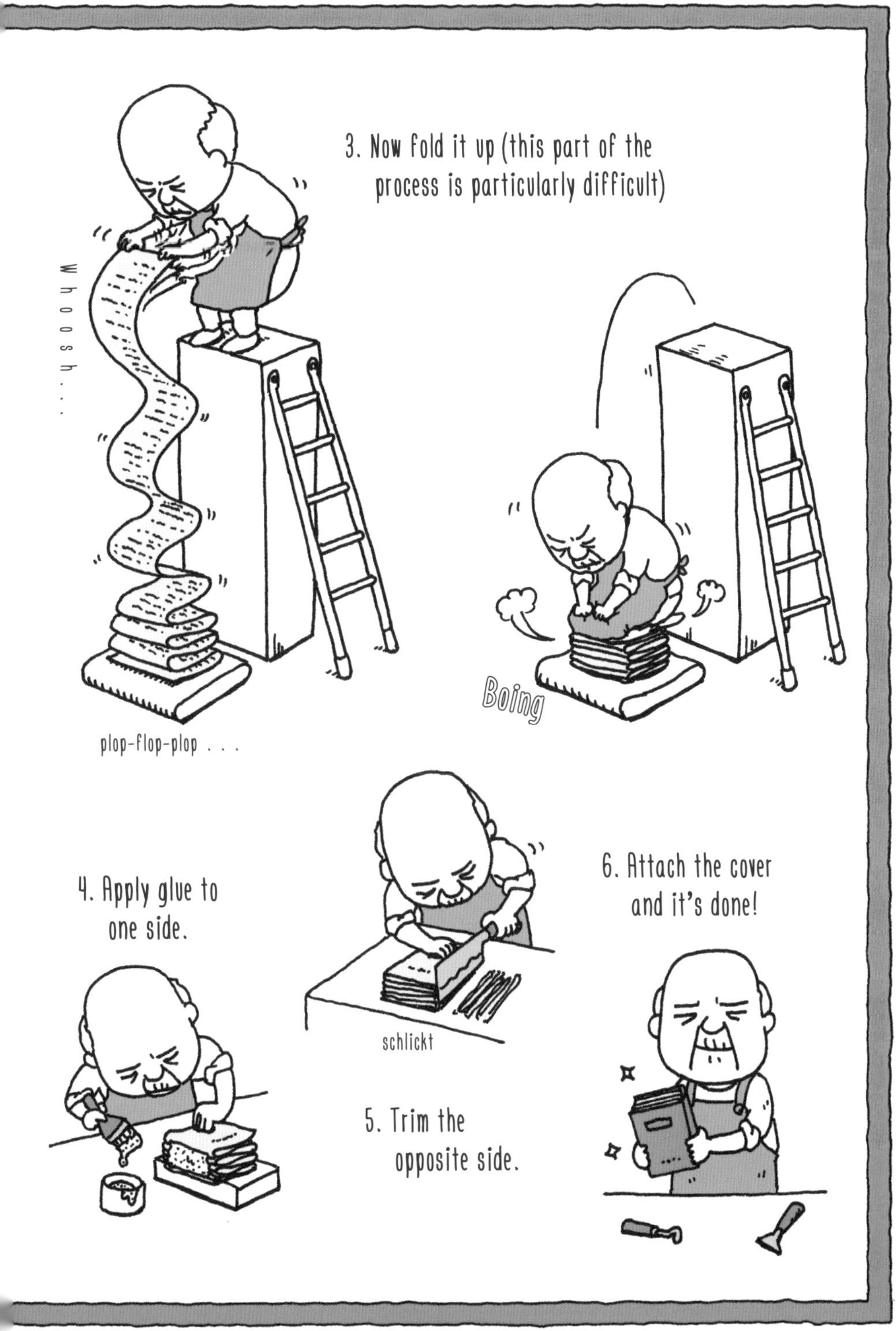
3. Now fold it up (this part of the process is particularly difficult)
Whoosh...
plop-flop-plop . . .
Boing
4. Apply glue to one side.
schlickt
5. Trim the opposite side.
6. Attach the cover and it's done!

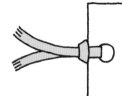

"WHERE BOOKS END UP"

1. Books that have been read to the point of falling apart go to the Book Recycling Center.

2. There the books are separated into their basic elements.

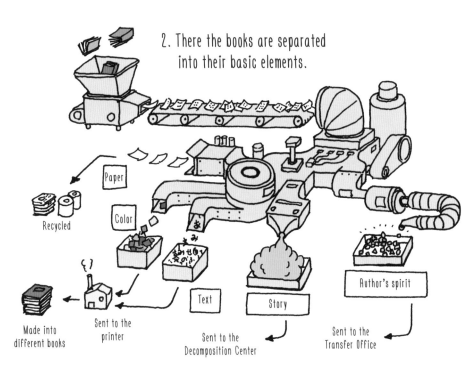

Paper

Recycled

Color

Text

Story

Author's spirit

Made into different books

Sent to the printer

Sent to the Decomposition Center

Sent to the Transfer Office

3. The story is taken to the Decomposition Center where it is further broken down into raw feelings.

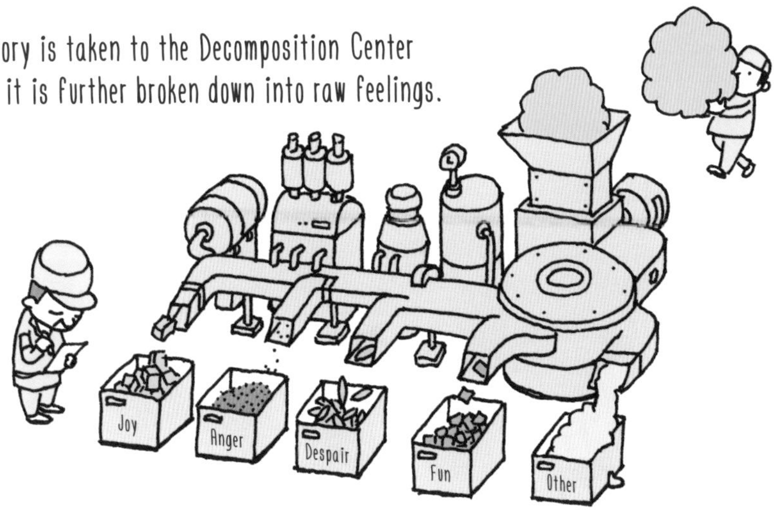
Joy
Anger
Despair
Fun
Other

4. The various "feelings" are scattered from the sky . . . . . . placed in nooks and crannies on streets . . . . . . and mixed in with additives and flavors . . .

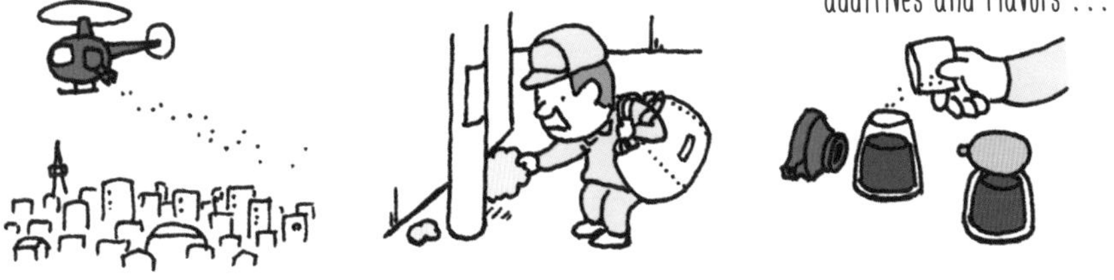

. . . so that they once again are blended into society.

5. The author's spirit is entrusted to specialists and secretly transferred to a future writer.

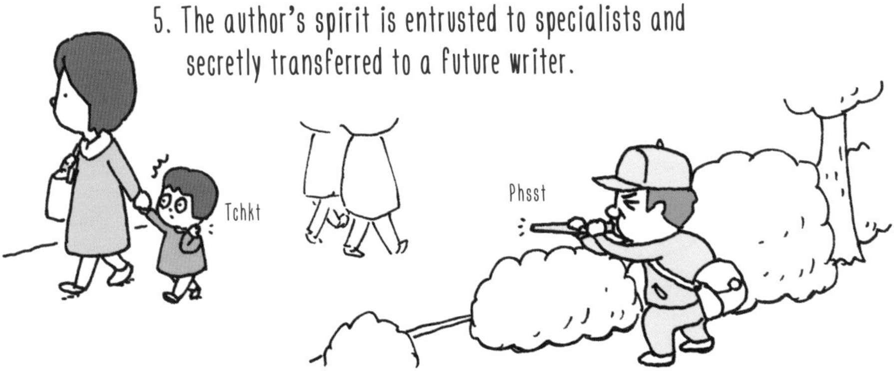
Tchkt
Phsst

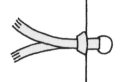

"PEOPLE WHO LIKE BOOKS"

What are your interests?

Well, I like books!

The statement "I like books" can have various meanings.

Likes to insert stuff into books

Sniff

Likes to smell books

Likes to peek at others' books

Likes to stack books

Likes to read books

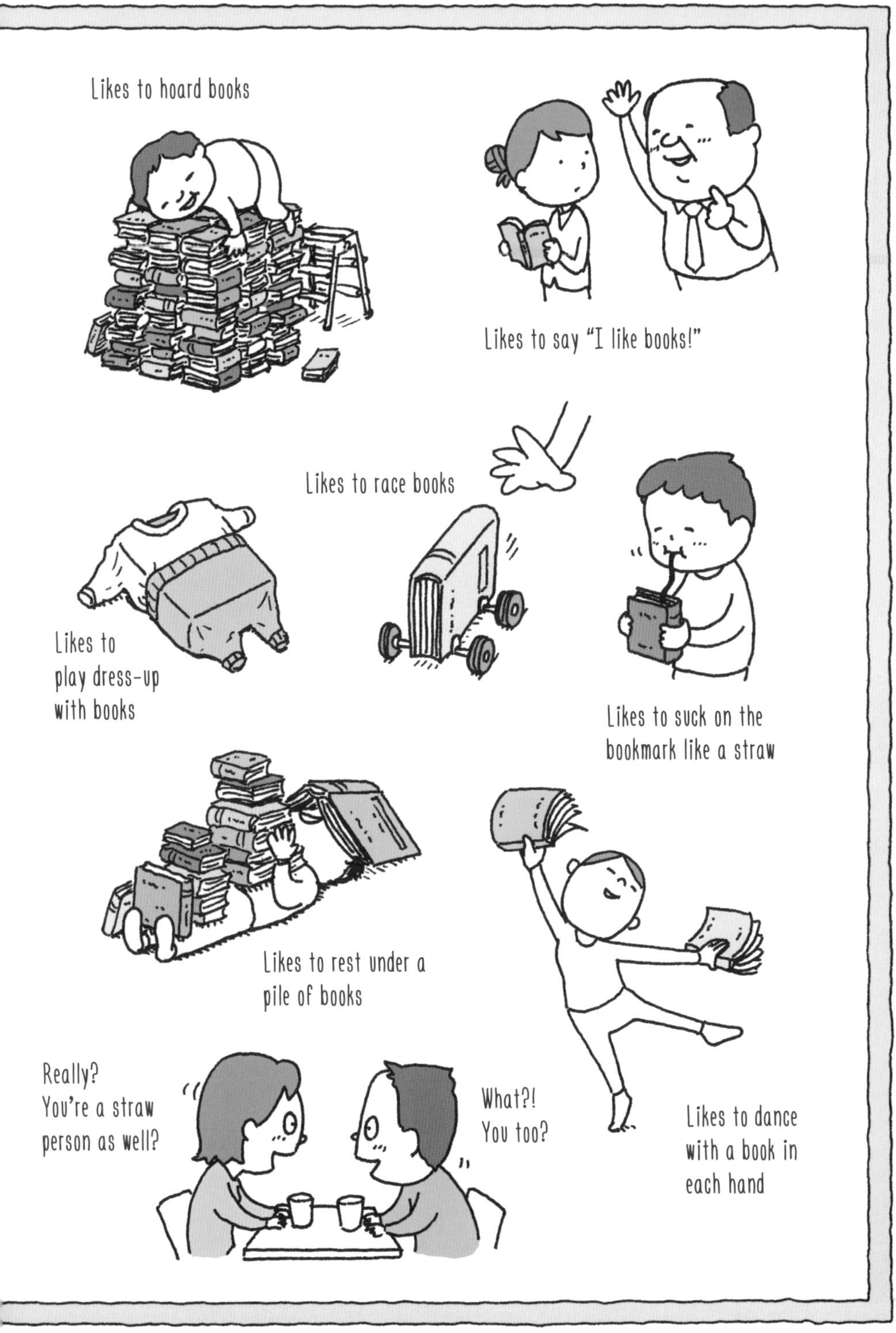

Likes to hoard books
Likes to say "I like books!"
Likes to race books
Likes to play dress-up with books
Likes to suck on the bookmark like a straw
Likes to rest under a pile of books
Likes to dance with a book in each hand
Really? You're a straw person as well?
What?! You too?

"THE PAGE-A-YEAR BOOK"

1. It's unknown when this very old and mysterious book was written.

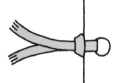

2. The pages are stuck together because of a special ink, and unless each page is carefully peeled away, the paper will rip and it won't be possible to turn every page.

The painstaking task of turning each page is incredibly slow, and can only be done at a rate of one page per year.

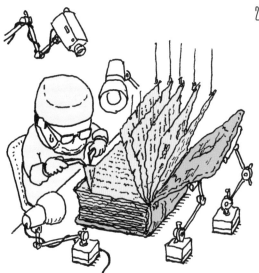

3. Having decoded the book's unique language, researchers have discovered that it is a book about the future, and accurately describes what has occurred in our world up until now.

4. They predict that if the pages continue to be turned at the current pace, in 50 years' time it will be possible to begin reading pages foretelling our future.

5. Judging by the thickness of the book, it is estimated that it might foretell the future for the next 2,000 years. It is hoped that technology will soon be developed that will speed up the pace of page-turning.

Rip!

TEST

Arghh! I can't take it anymore!

I want to rip it to bits!

6. The task of page-turning is incredibly stressful, and no matter how dedicated the turner is, five years is usually as long as anyone can handle such work.

"THE SOLITARY STORYBOOK"

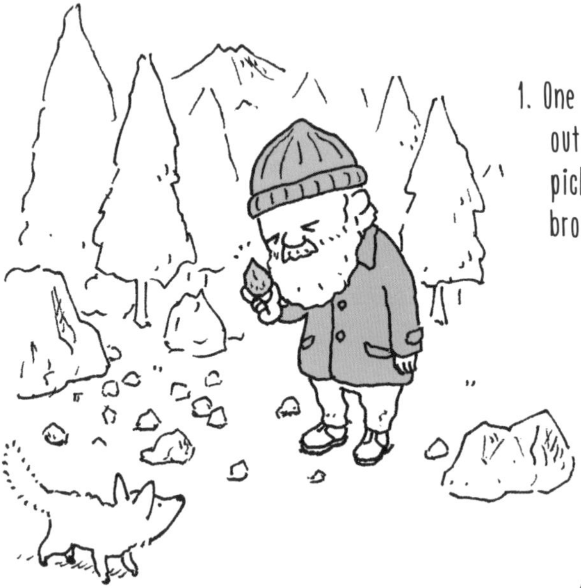

1. One day an old man went out for a morning walk, picked up a rock, and brought it home.

2. That afternoon he gazed at the rock. He gave it a name and made up a story in which the rock featured as the main character.

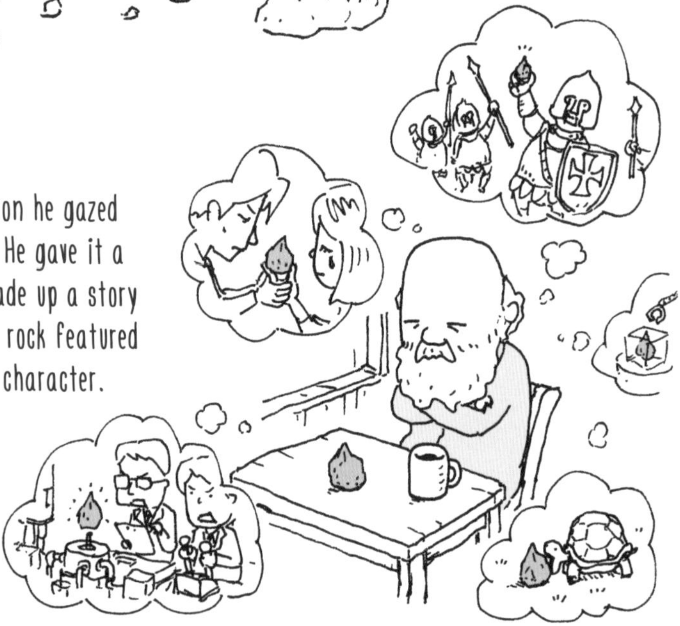

3. When night came, he opened his notebook and wrote about the rock and its story.

4. The next morning he returned the rock to where he found it.

5. He picked up another rock and brought it home.

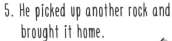

6. As days went by, the notebook became a book of stories.

7. This book, which he had written only for himself, was buried with him when he died.

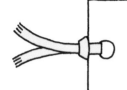

"BOOK PEOPLE"

1. We are all like books.

2. We all have our own story, but just looking at us won't reveal what is inside.

3. We are always waiting for someone to discover us, and always hoping someone will look inside.

4. Some of us are popular, while others aren't. But if someone pleasantly discovers us, we can change each other's lives.

5. Once we've been discovered, we can share a wonderful moment together.

6. We are bulky and heavy, we can be damaged by fire and water. Our cover fades over time, and we can be wrinkled.

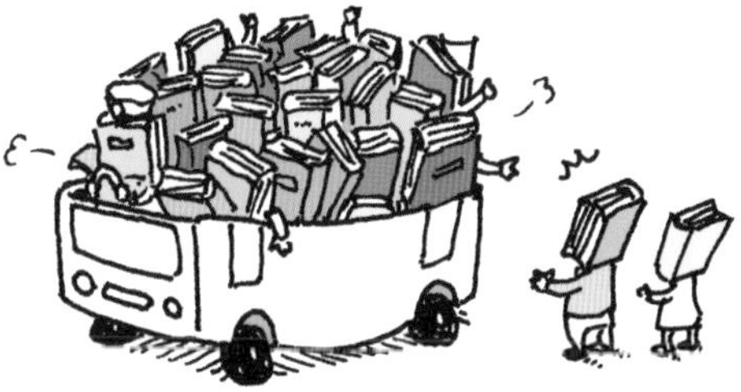

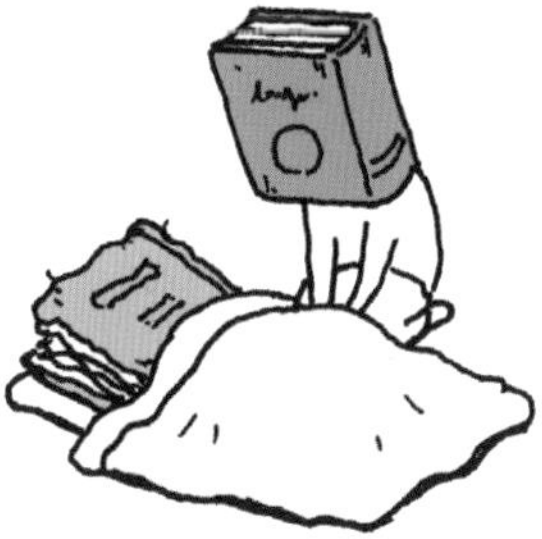

7. We are physical things with a finite lifespan, but we can pass along our spirit.

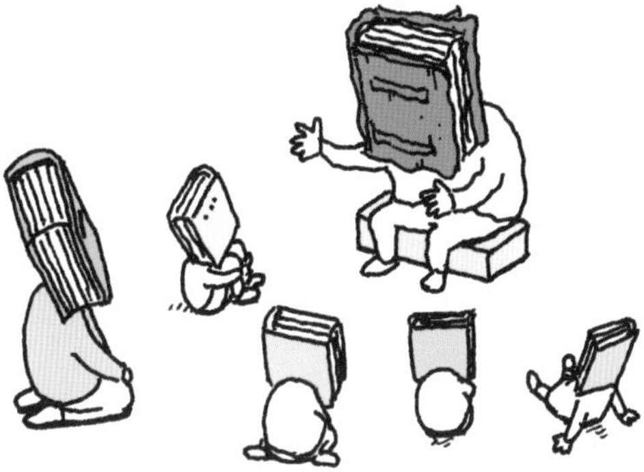

8. We start off new and unknown, and then over time we add our story to the world.

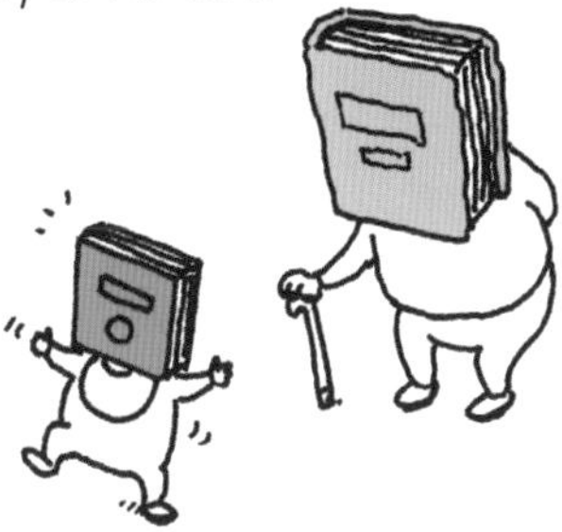

9. That is why we . . .

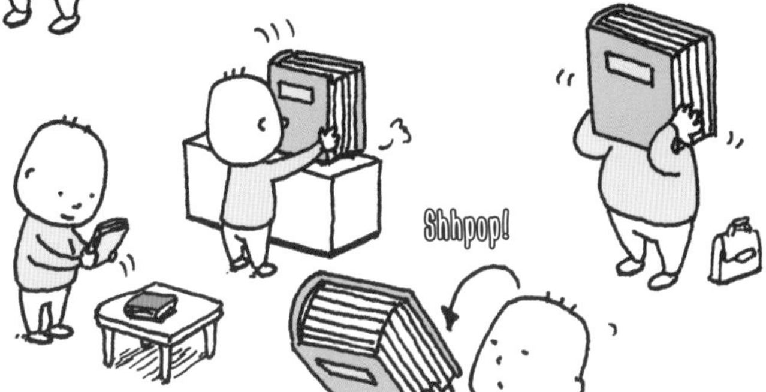

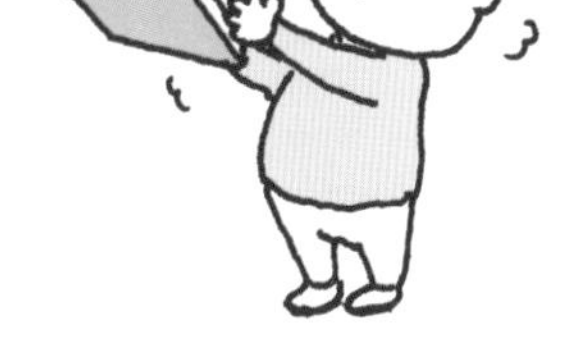
Shhpop!

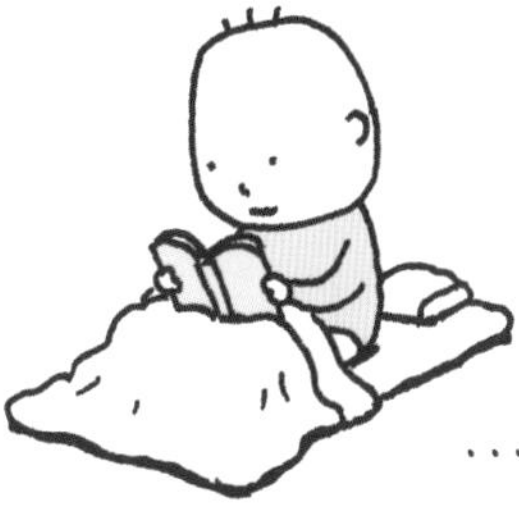

. . . love books.

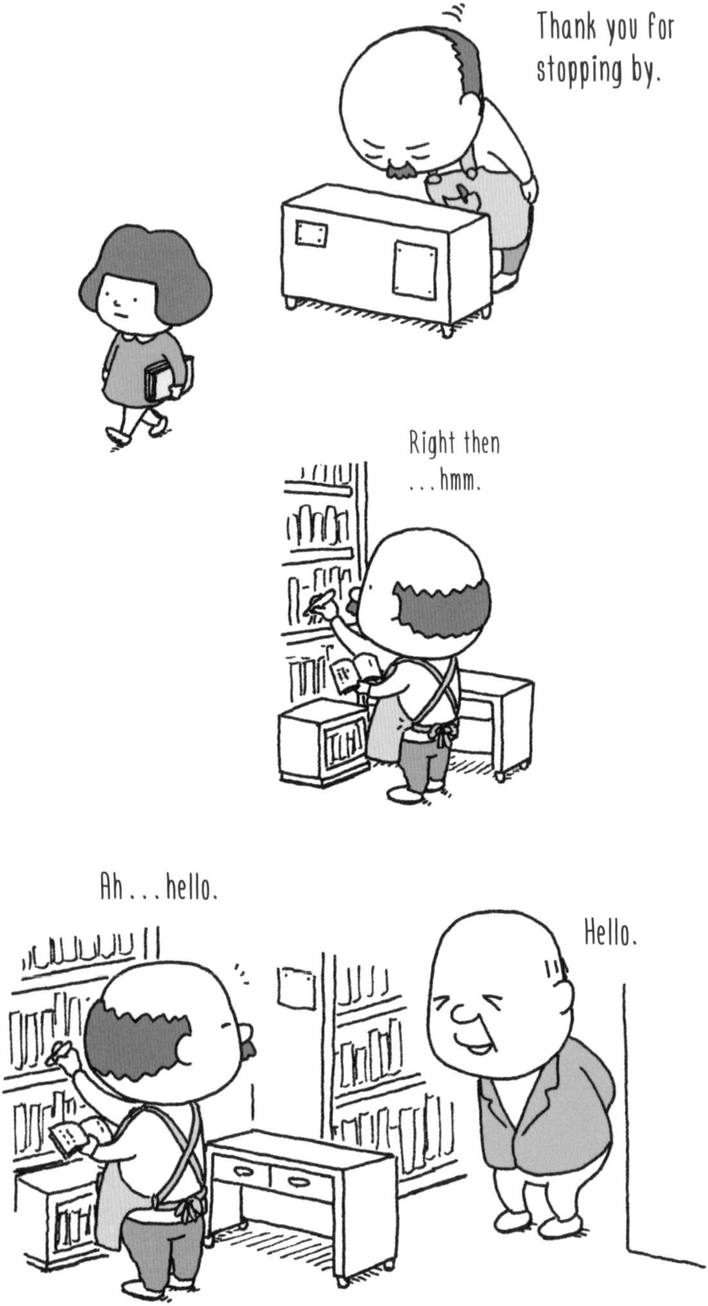
Thank you for
stopping by.
Right then
. . . hmm.
Ah . . . hello.
Hello.

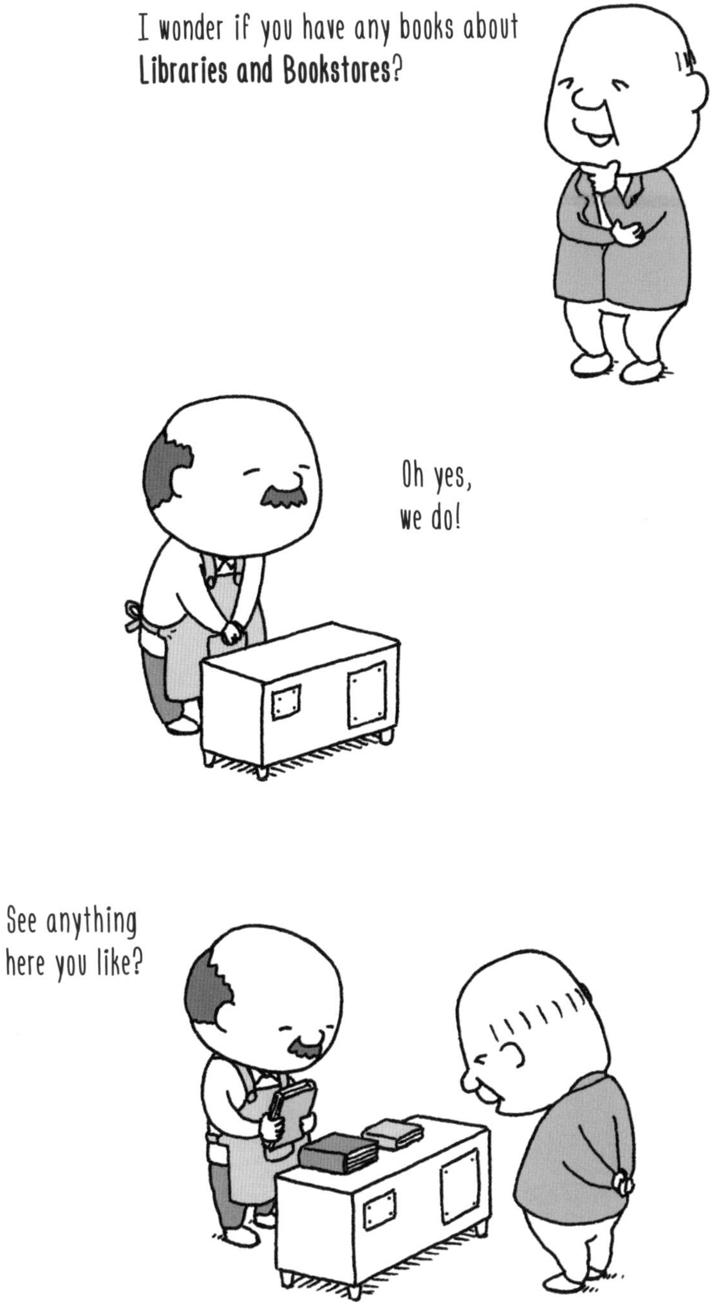
I wonder if you have any books about **Libraries and Bookstores**?
Oh yes, we do!
See anything here you like?

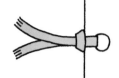

"THE BEAUTY OF LIBRARIES VOLUME I"

The books on someone's bookcase belong to that person alone.

But the books in libraries have dreams to share with everyone.

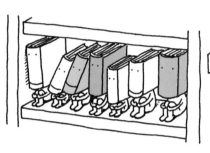

"I might become useful to someone."

"I might be able to entertain or cheer someone up."

"I might be able to spark someone's interests or bring people together."

Until the special day when someone reads them, these books wait on their shelves with these hopes held between their pages

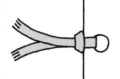

"THE BEAUTY OF LIBRARIES VOLUME II"

Whoever first dreamed up the idea of a library must have felt a thrill of happiness like no one ever had before.

He must have thought, "We need a place where anyone can read the stories and knowledge of the entire world to their heart's content!" He must have known the joy this would bring.

He would have lain awake at night, sleepless with the excitement of such a rare and wonderful idea.

"THE BEAUTY OF LIBRARIES VOLUME III"

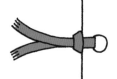

It would be nice to be able to ask the returned books:

How did it go?

Were you read earnestly?

Was there laughter while you were read? Or tears?

What other books did they have in the house?

Whom would you like to read you next?

But the books are discreet,

Shh

Shh

they always come home to the library without revealing a thing.

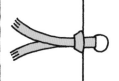

"THE BEAUTY OF LIBRARIES VOLUME IV"

A meeting place for people living now and people who lived long ago

A place for people just starting their life, and for those who have lived a long life

A place to go to be alone

A place for people who find comfort in the company of others

A place for people who take pride in saying, "I went to the library"

A place for people who love books

A place for people who like "people who love books"

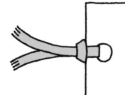

"WHAT KIND OF PLACE IS A BOOKSTORE?"

The pros

1. A bookstore is home to those pros who know how:
   to introduce a good book to someone;
   to give a good book a future;
   to help new books come into this world.

2. It is a place where money can buy those things that money cannot buy, such as hopes, disappointments and desires; lives lived by others, unseen landscapes, the secrets of the world, a whole new perspective and sense of self.

3. It is a place where you can always discover new worlds that cannot be found online.

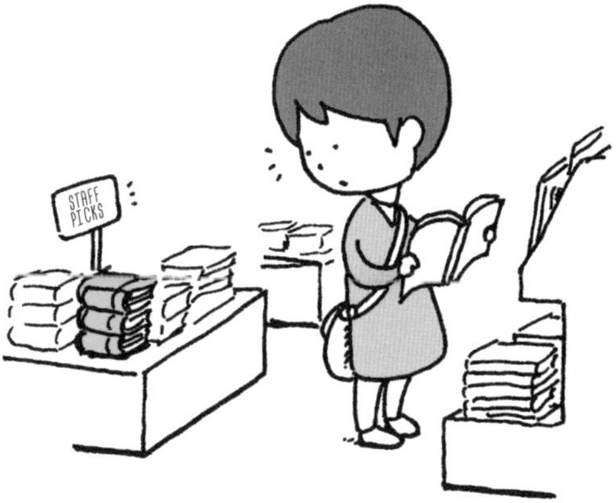
STAFF PICKS

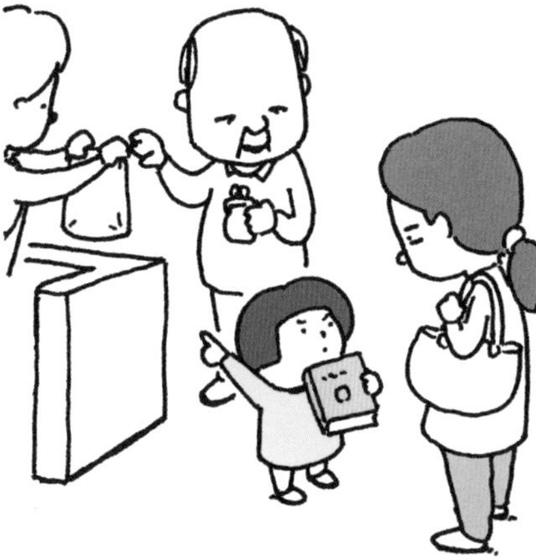

4. It is a place where investments are made in readers who will create future masterworks.

5. It is a place where there will always be room for new books.

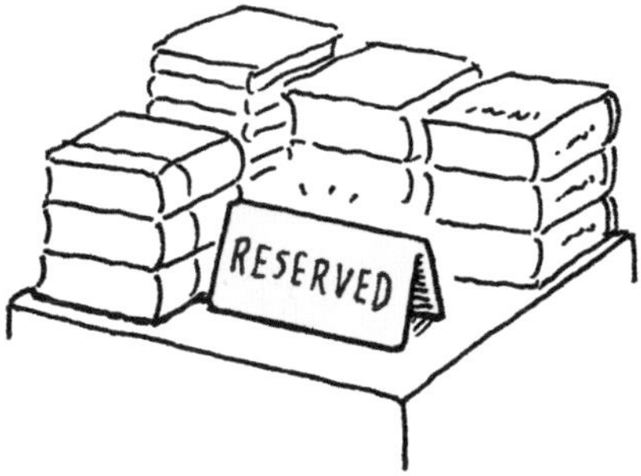
RESERVED

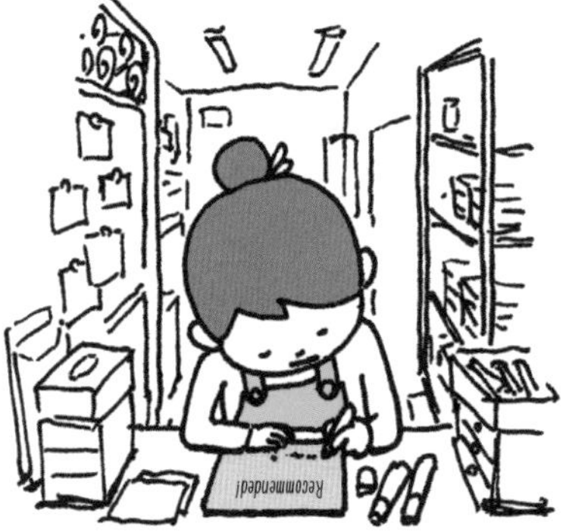
Recommended!

6. It is a place where people who have been helped by books can work to express their gratitude to books.

Oh, yes . . . yes!
I see . . . I see.

Um, I once read book
many years ago about a
mobile bookstore . . .

A mobile bookstore . . . ?
Hmm . . .

. . . Ah!

I wonder if it might
be this one?

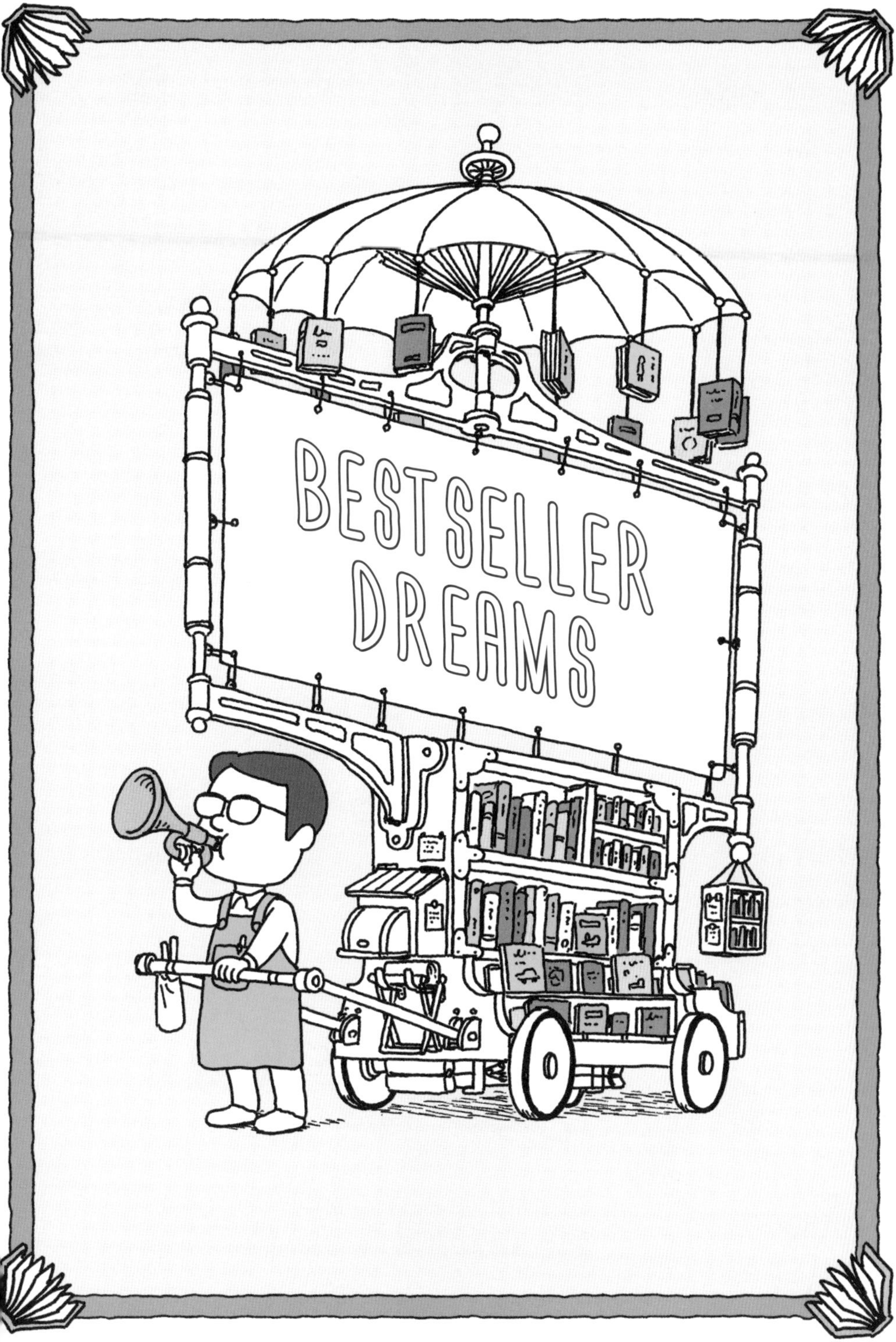
BESTSELLER
DREAMS

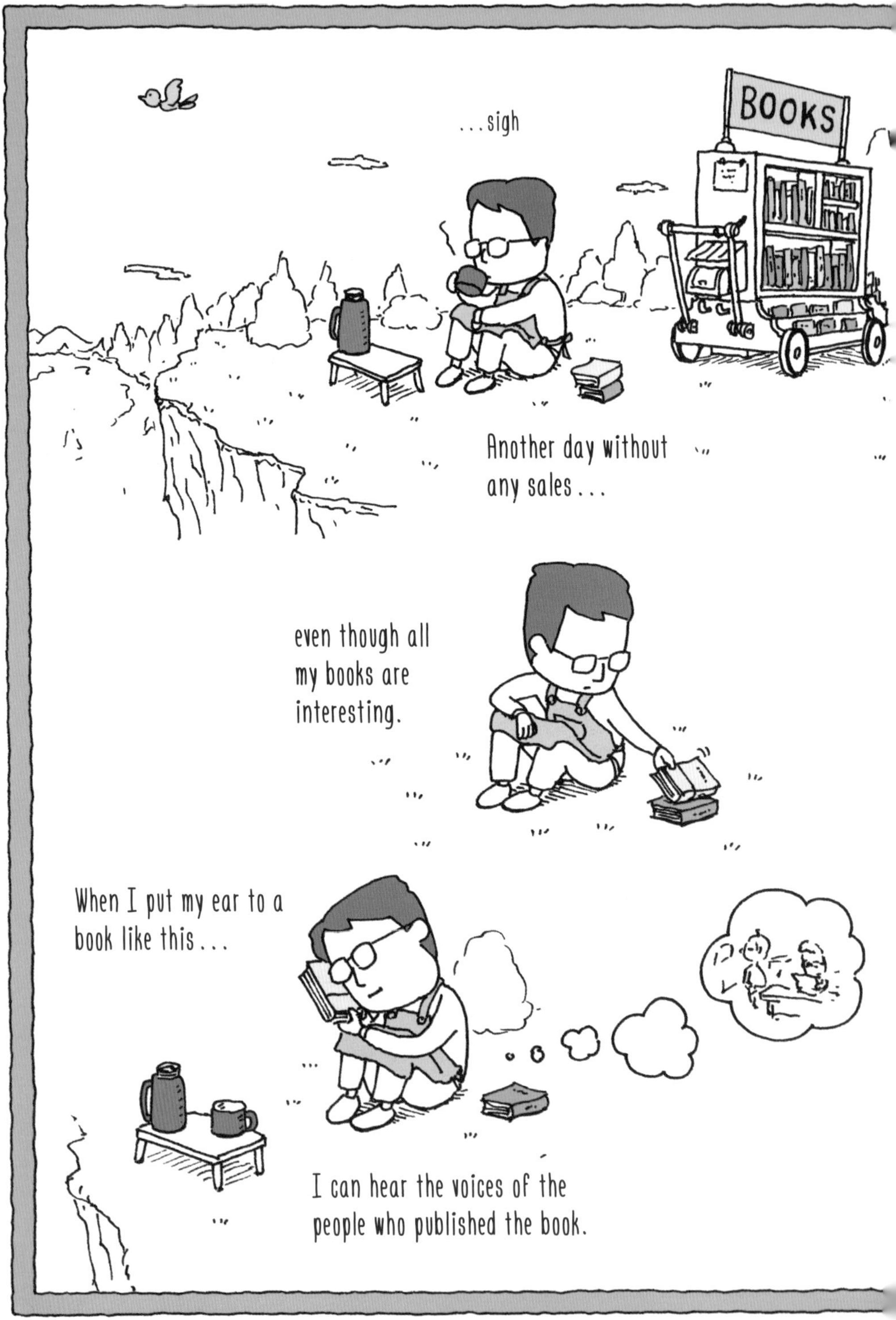
...sigh
BOOKS
Another day without any sales...
even though all my books are interesting.
When I put my ear to a book like this...
I can hear the voices of the people who published the book.

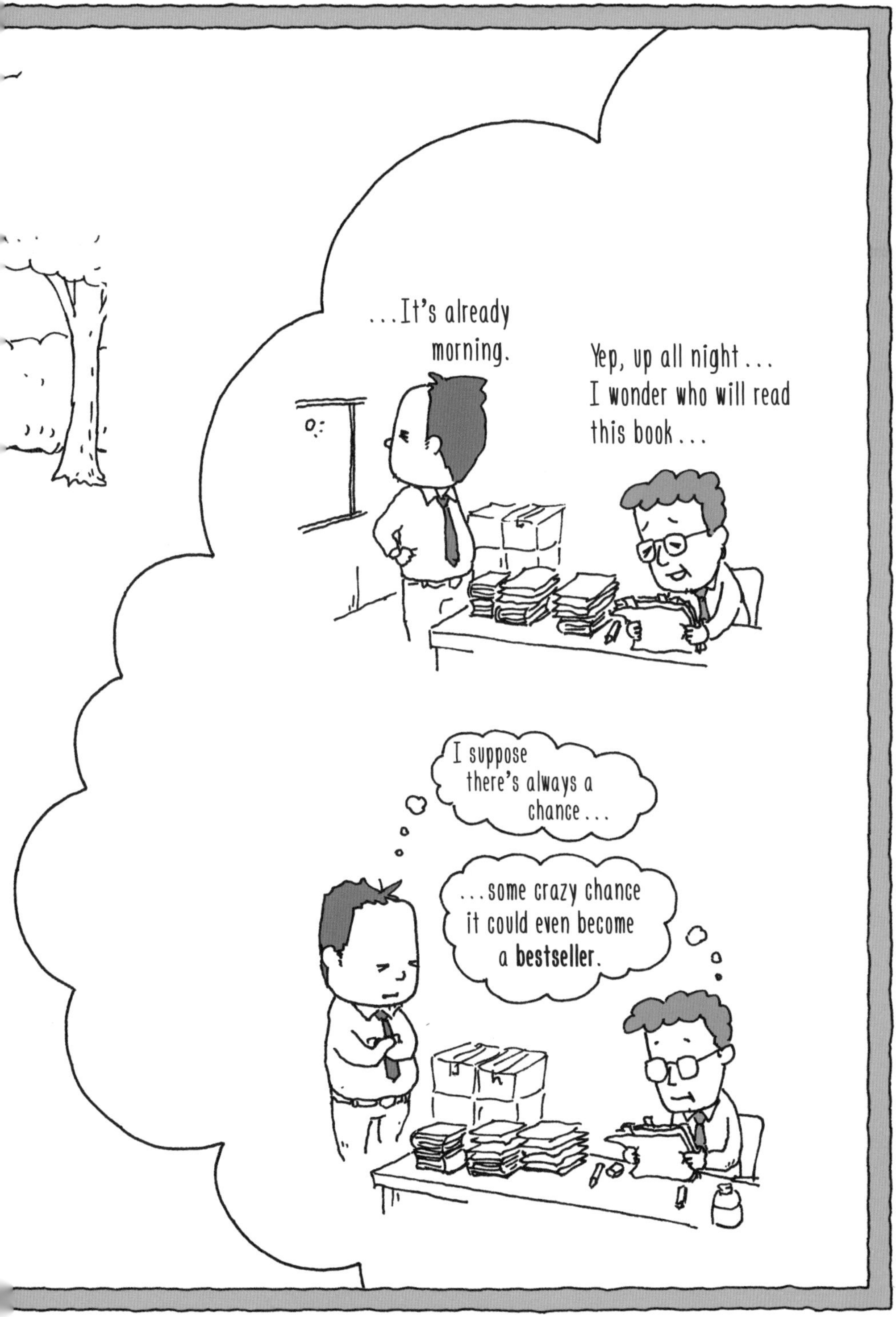
...It's already morning.
Yep, up all night... I wonder who will read this book...
I suppose there's always a chance...
...some crazy chance it could even become a **bestseller**.

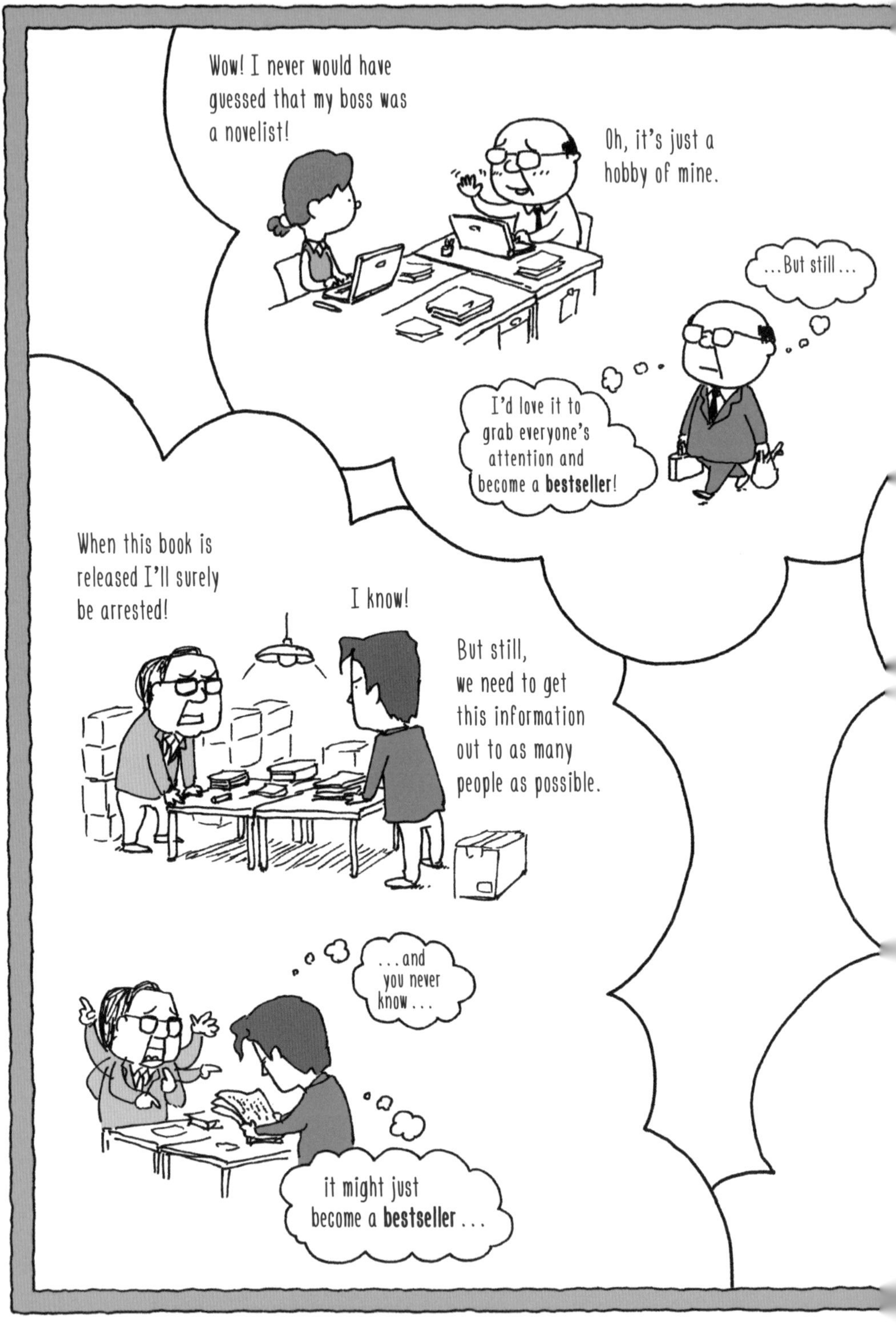
Wow! I never would have guessed that my boss was a novelist!
Oh, it's just a hobby of mine.
...But still...
I'd love it to grab everyone's attention and become a **bestseller**!
When this book is released I'll surely be arrested!
I know!
But still, we need to get this information out to as many people as possible.
...and you never know...
it might just become a **bestseller**...

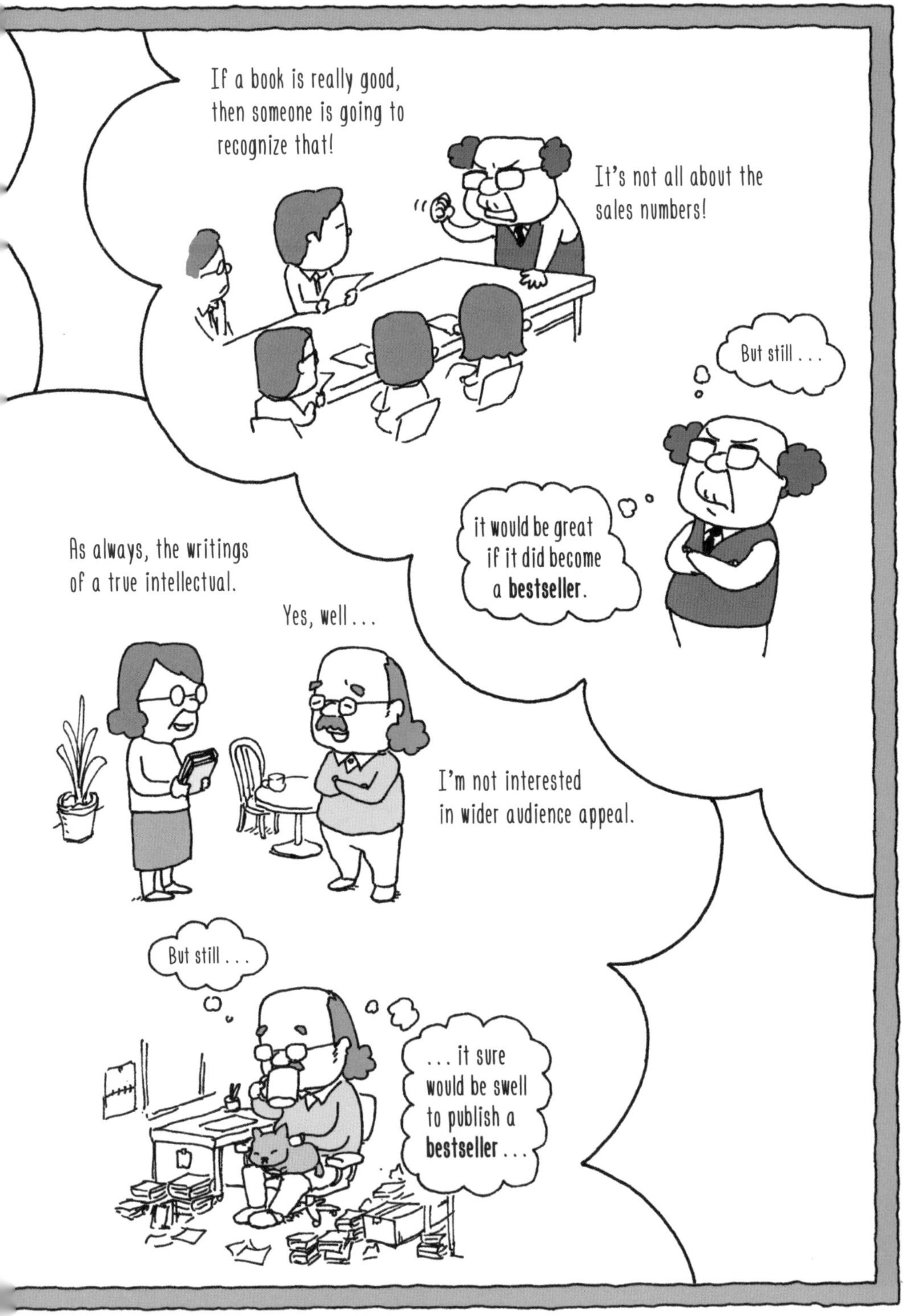
If a book is really good, then someone is going to recognize that!
It's not all about the sales numbers!
But still . . .
it would be great if it did become a **bestseller**.
As always, the writings of a true intellectual.
Yes, well . . .
I'm not interested in wider audience appeal.
But still . . .
. . . it sure would be swell to publish a **bestseller** . . .

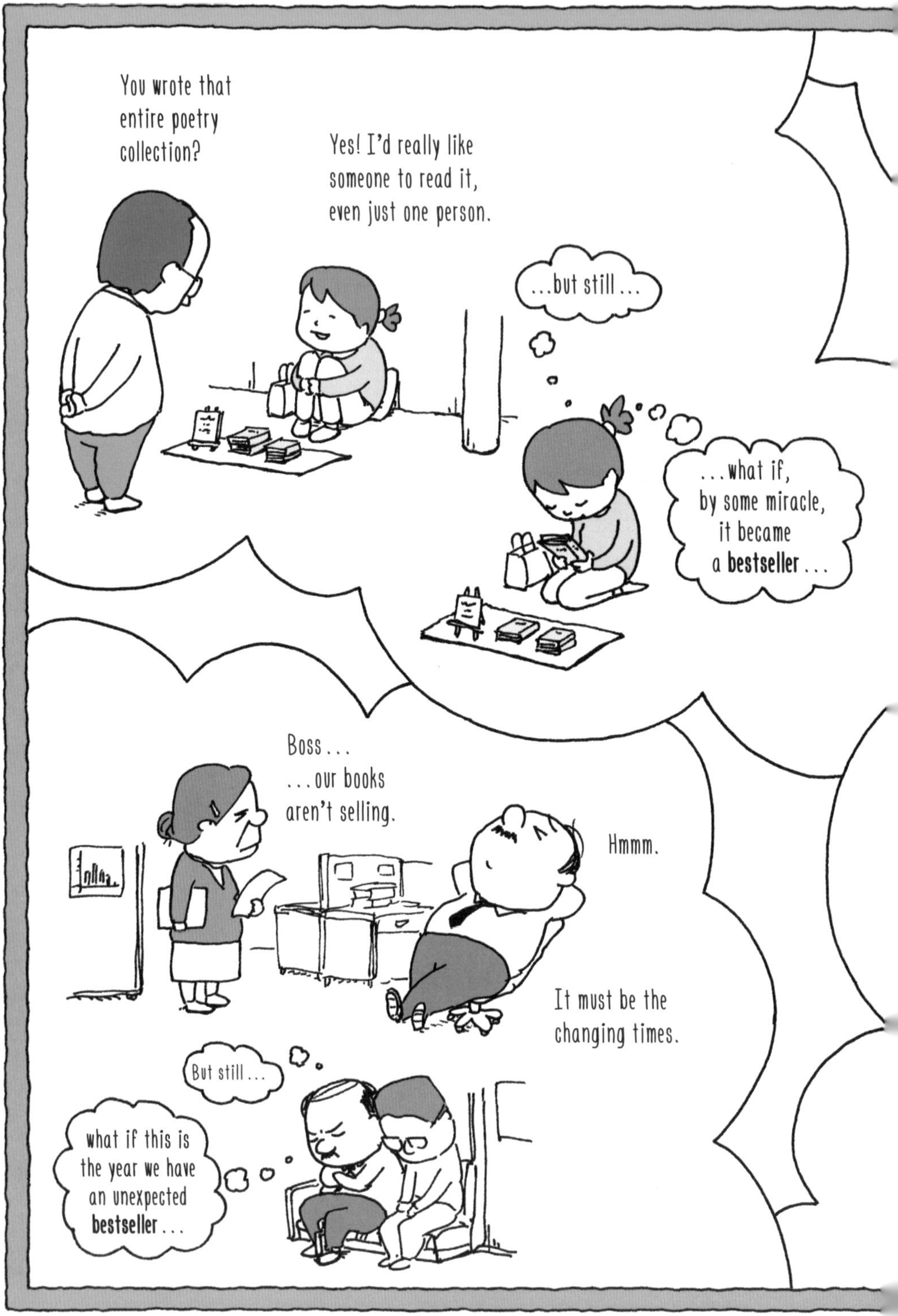
You wrote that entire poetry collection?
Yes! I'd really like someone to read it, even just one person.
...but still...
...what if, by some miracle, it became a **bestseller**...
Boss...
...our books aren't selling.
Hmmm.
It must be the changing times.
But still...
what if this is the year we have an unexpected **bestseller**...

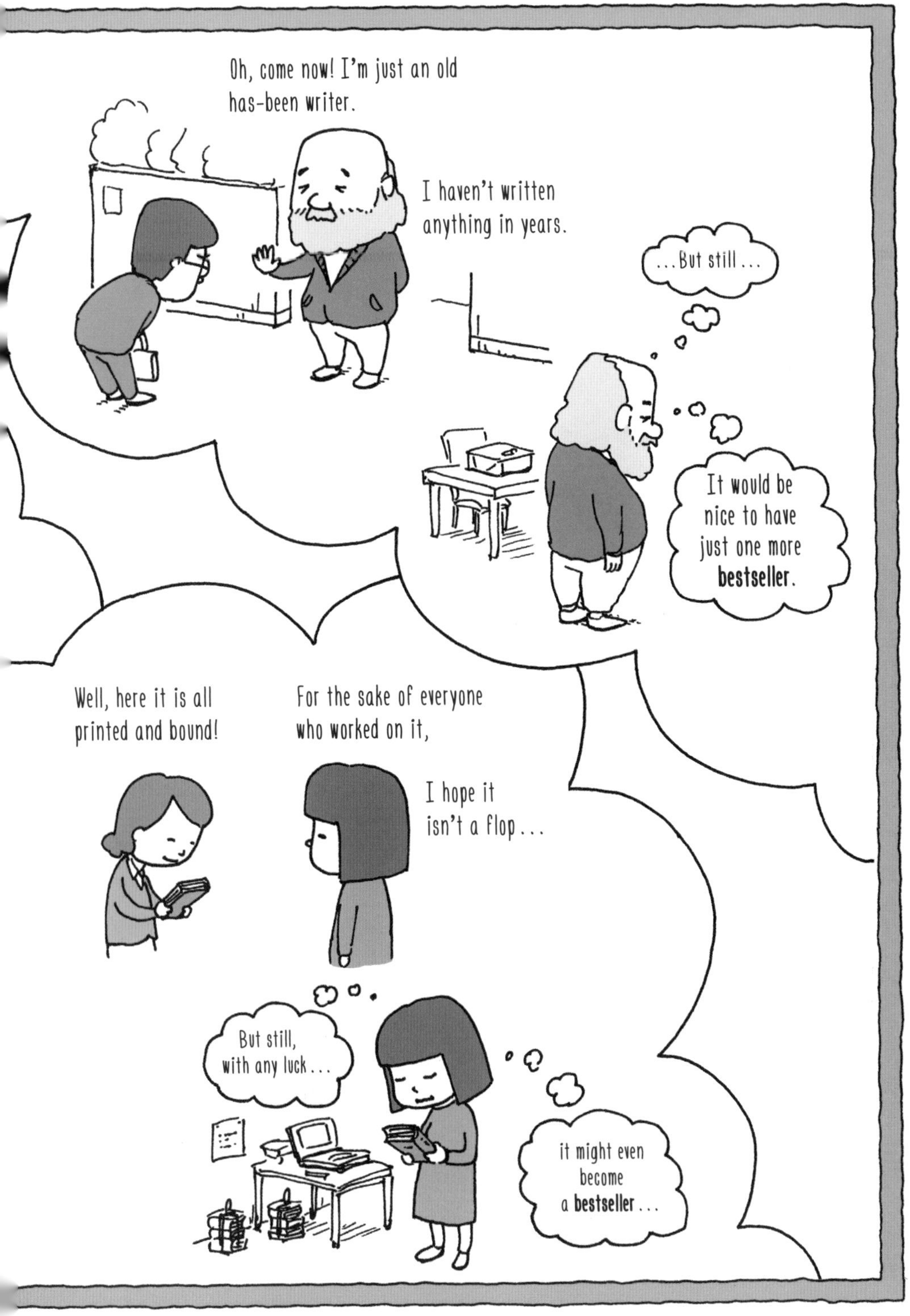

Oh, come now! I'm just an old has-been writer.
I haven't written anything in years.
...But still...
It would be nice to have just one more **bestseller**.
Well, here it is all printed and bound!
For the sake of everyone who worked on it,
I hope it isn't a flop...
But still, with any luck...
it might even become a **bestseller**...

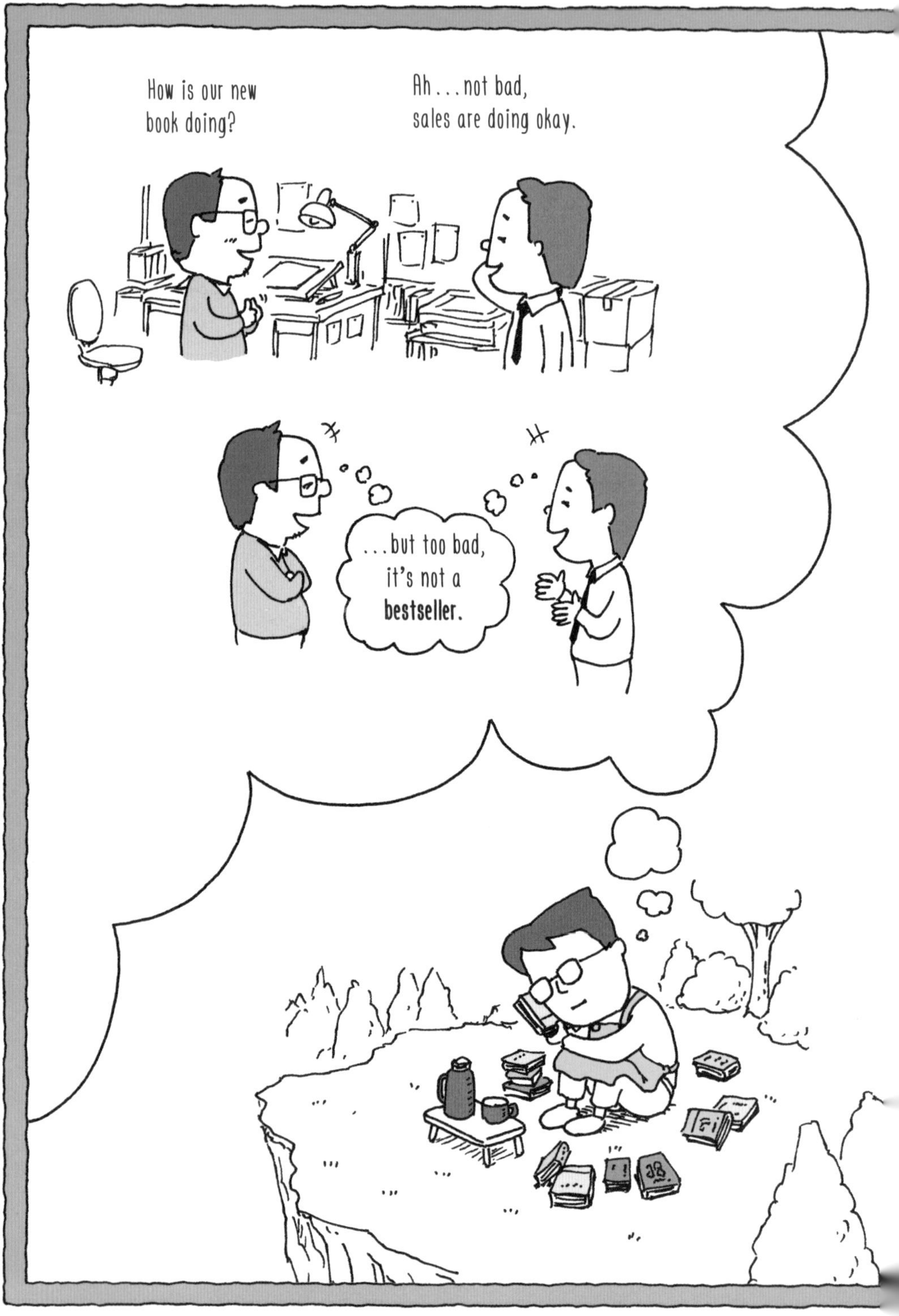
How is our new book doing?
Ah . . . not bad, sales are doing okay.
. . . but too bad, it's not a **bestseller.**

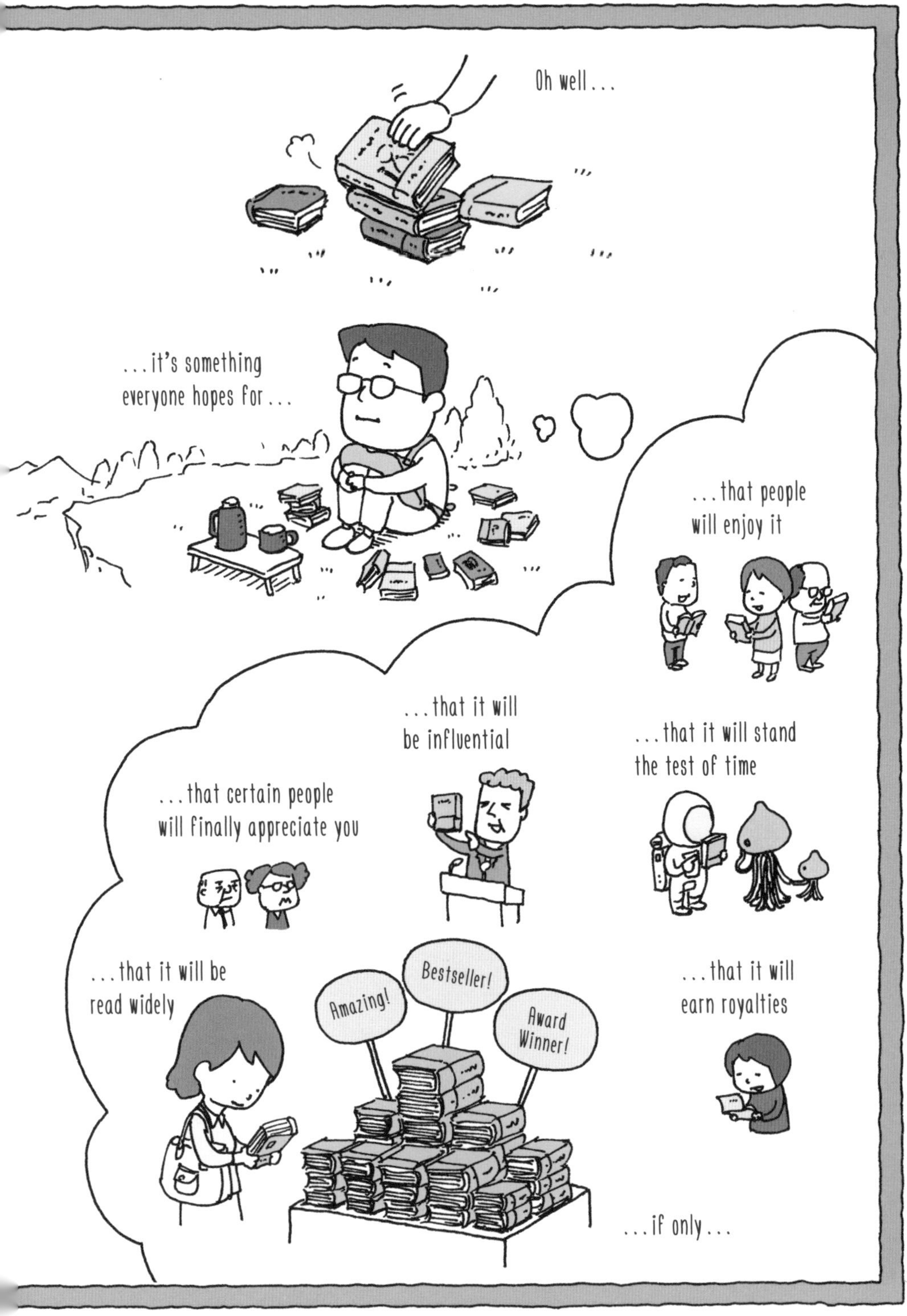

Oh well...
...it's something everyone hopes for...
...that people will enjoy it
...that it will be influential
...that it will stand the test of time
...that certain people will finally appreciate you
...that it will be read widely
Amazing!
Bestseller!
Award Winner!
...that it will earn royalties
...if only...

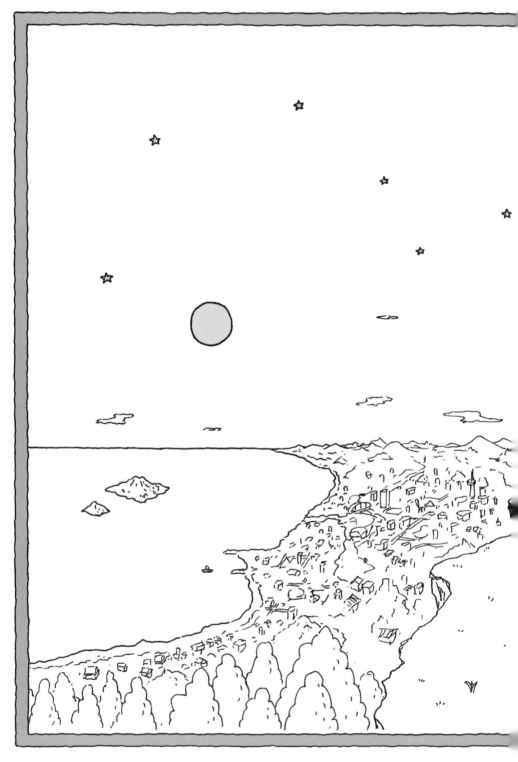

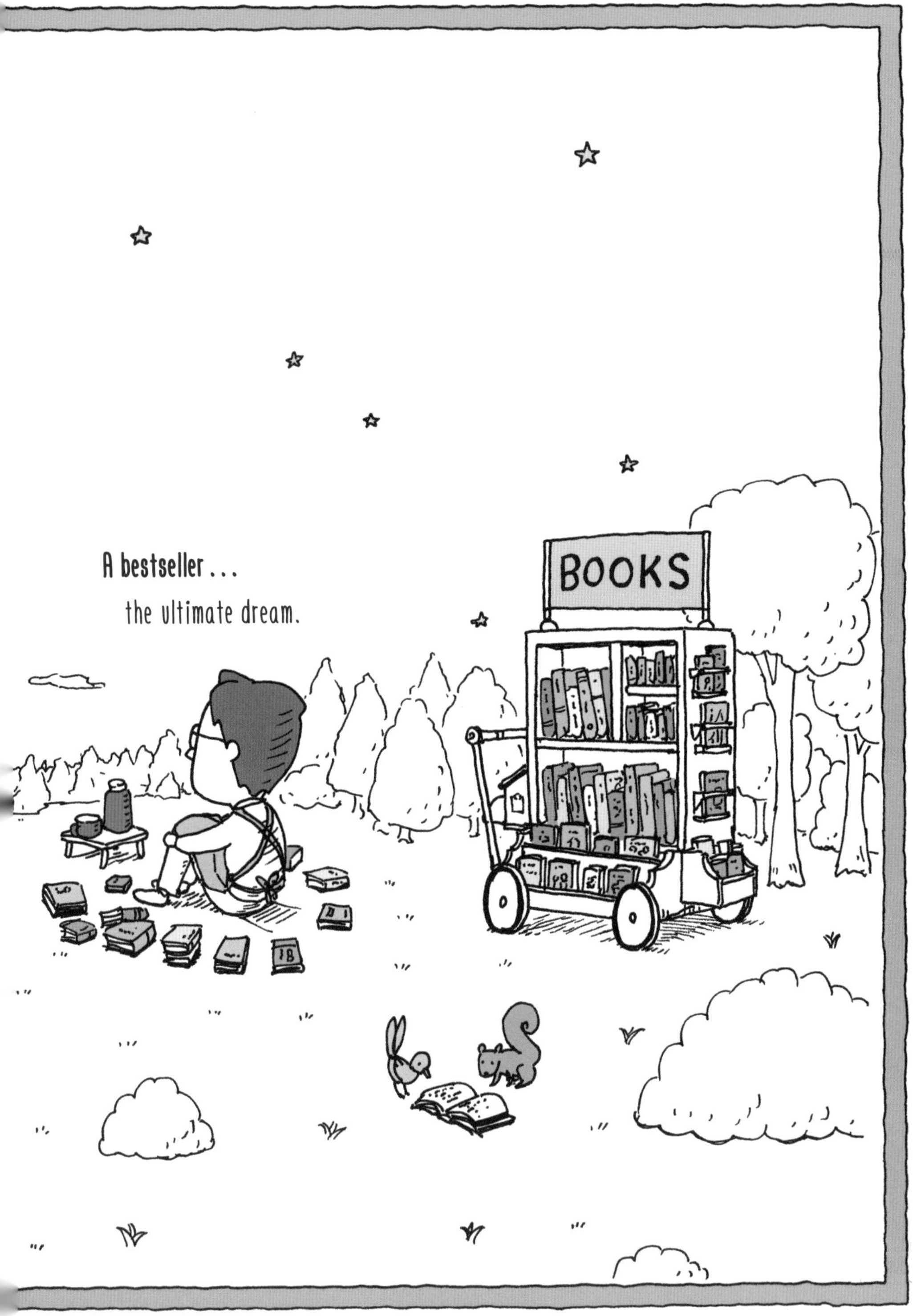
A bestseller . . .
the ultimate dream.
BOOKS

Yes!
That's the one!
I've finally
found it again.

Oh, that's
wonderful!
How nice!

I can't thank
you enough...

No no,
thank you.

Ahh.
Books are so
interesting...

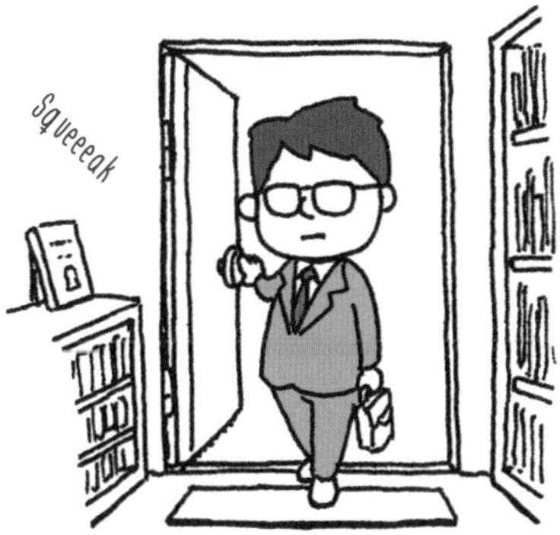
Squeeeak

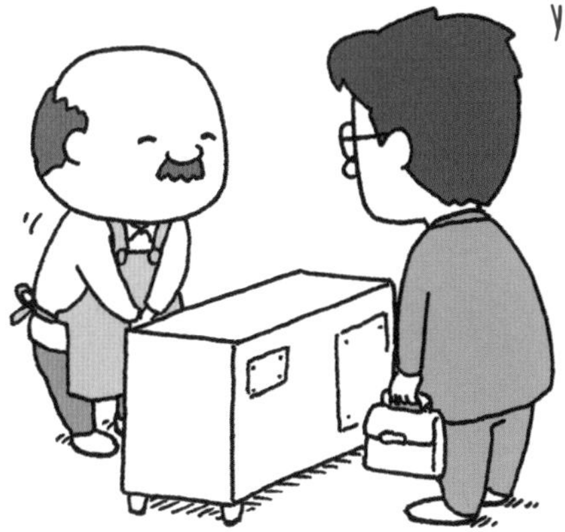
Um, excuse me, but I heard about
your special bookstore.
Aha, I see.
Welcome!

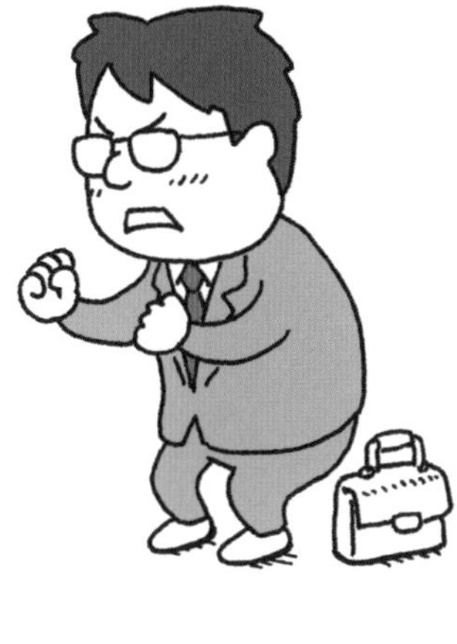
Um . . . I wonder if you
have any books about
**the surefire way to
create a bestseller?**

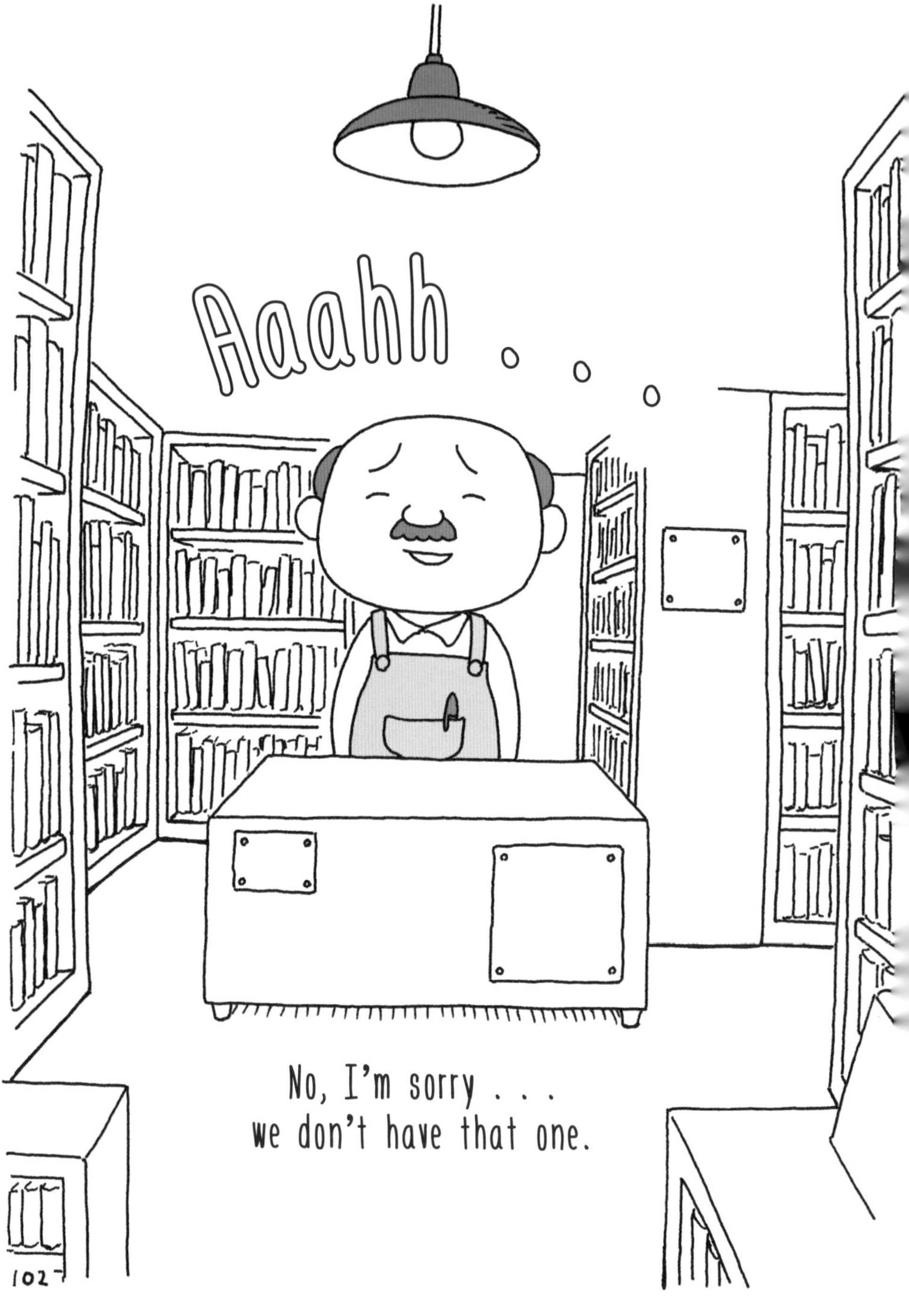
Aaahh . . .
No, I'm sorry . . .
we don't have that one.

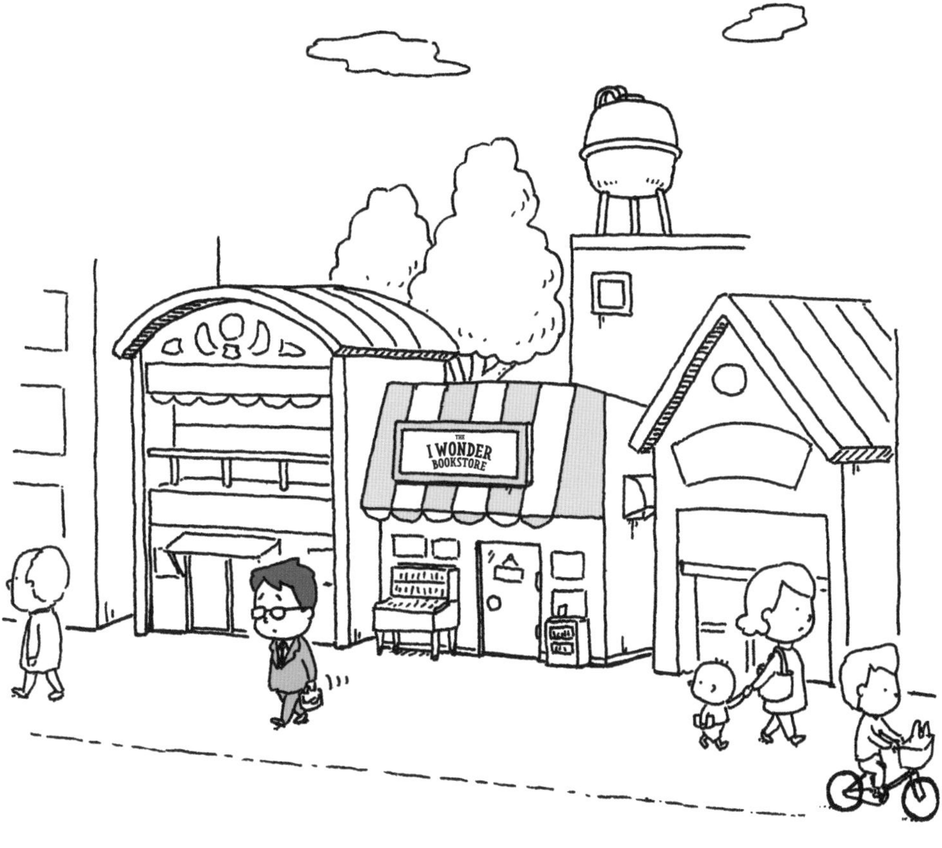
THE
I WONDER
BOOKSTORE

THE END.

About the Author

Born in Kanagawa Prefecture in 1973, Shinsuke Yoshitake earned a graduate degree in Plastic Art and Mixed Media from the School of Art & Design of University of Tsukuba. He received first place in the sixth MOE Picture Book Award and Art Prize of the 61st Sankei Children's Book Award for *Ringo Kamoshirenai* (*It Might Be an Apple*), first place in the eighth MOE Picture Book Award for *Riyu ga Arimasu* (*I Have a Reason*), first place in the ninth MOE Picture Book Award and a Special Mention Bologna Ragazzi Award for *Mou Nugenai* (*Still Stuck*), and won the 51st Shinpu Award for *Konoato Doushichaou* (*What Happens Next?*). Father of two, he is the author of many other books.

The I Wonder Bookstore
by Shinsuke Yoshitake

Arukashira Shoten
by Shinsuke Yoshitake
Copyright © Shinsuke Yoshitake 2017
First published in the United States in 2019
by Chronicle Books LLC.

Original Japanese edition published in 2017
by POPLAR Publishing Co., Ltd.
This English-language edition is published by
rights and production arrangement with
POPLAR Publishing Co., Ltd., Tokyo, Japan,
through Pont Cerise llc
and Rico Komanoya; Tokyo, Japan.

Library of Congress Cataloging-in-Publication Data
Names: Yoshitake, Shinsuke, 1973 - author, illustrator.
Title: The I Wonder Bookstore / Shinsuke Yoshitake.
Other titles: *Arukashira shoten*. English
Description: San Francisco : Chronicle Books, [2019] | Translation of:
Arukashira shoten. | Summary: A whimsical look inside the I Wonder Bookstore where the customers
search for such treasures as the book that can only be read by moonlight and other rather rare books.
Identifiers: LCCN 2018013373 | ISBN 9781452176512 (hardcover : alk. paper)
Subjects: LCSH: Books and reading—Juvenile fiction. | Bookstores—Juvenile fiction. | Humorous stories. | Graphic novels. |
CYAC: Graphic novels. | Books and reading—Fiction. | Bookstores—Fiction. | Humorous stories. | LCGFT: Humorous fiction.
Classification: LCC PZ7.7.Y67 Iam 2019 | DDC 741.5/952—dc23 LC record available at https://lccn.loc.gov/2018013373

Manufactured in China

Book Design: bookwall, Andrew Pothecary (itsumo music)
English translation: Geoffrey Trousselot
Editing: Saori Fujita, Rico Komanoya, Steven Mockus
Production: Aki Ueda (Pont Cerise)

10 9 8 7 6 5 4 3

Chronicle Books LLC, 680 Second Street
San Francisco CA 94107
www.chroniclebooks.com